THE SECRET OF WILDCAT SWAMP

An invitation from Cap Bailey, science teacher at
Bayport High, to accompany him out West to Wildcat Swamp on an archaeological expedition triggers
off a series of dangerous events for Frank and Joe
Hardy.

Just before they leave, a ruthless criminal breaks
out of prison. Their famous detective father, who is
tracking down a gang of freight-train robbers, suspects the escapee is part of the gang. Investigation
leads him to believe that the robbers might be hiding
out in Wildcat Swamp!

On their way West the boys and Cap have a near-
fatal accident in a private plane which has been sabo-
taged. When they start digging for fossils, a giant
boulder comes hurtling straight toward them as if
guided by an invisible hand. Though warned to
leave the area, Frank, Joe, and Cap doggedly remain
until they have caught the cunning ex-convicts they
are up against in this swift-paced adventure.

"Nice cave mates you pick for yourself!"
Frank remarked

Hardy Boys Mystery Stories

THE SECRET OF WILDCAT SWAMP

BY

FRANKLIN W. DIXON

NEW YORK
GROSSET & DUNLAP
Publishers

CONTENTS

CHAPTER		PAGE
I	PRISON BREAK	1
II	ESCAPE BY TRAIN	9
III	A HAZARDOUS TAKE-OFF	17
IV	FINGERPRINT TIP	24
V	INTO PERILOUS COUNTRY	31
VI	DEADLY DANGER	43
VII	SKELETONS AND SCHEMES	53
VIII	ORDERED OUT	65
IX	LOST!	73
X	THREE ODD LETTERS	82
XI	UNDERGROUND SNARE	90
XII	AMBUSH	97
XIII	AN ICY DUNGEON	104
XIV	THIEVES' CAMP	113
XV	THE WRECK	122
XVI	THE ROUGH RIDE	129
XVII	A FRIENDLY OUTLAW	138
XVIII	TRAPPED!	149
XIX	TO THE RESCUE	159
XX	THE ROUNDUP	171

CHAPTER I

Prison Break

"IF SOMEBODY doesn't toss a mystery our way, fellows, we may actually be swimming in this pool one of these days."

Frank and Joe Hardy stopped digging and leaned on their shovels. The boys grinned as they studied the perspiring, chubby face of Chet Morton.

"Shall we tell him, Joe?" Frank asked with an exaggerated lift of his eyebrows.

"Tell me what?" Chet demanded. "Aw, listen, fellows! Long before school closed for the summer you promised me you'd come out here to the farm and help me clean out this bog."

Eighteen-year-old Frank Hardy, with a wink at his brother, who was only a year younger, gazed thoughtfully at their best friend.

"Well, aren't we helping?" he said. "But how would you like to help us catch a couple of train robbers, Chet?"

"No kidding!" Joe added. "Last night Dad was talking about one of his cases, and said maybe we could help him."

The brothers, sons of Fenton Hardy, an internationally known private detective, frequently assisted their father. Their first mystery had been *The Tower Treasure,* and not long ago they had solved *The Wailing Siren Mystery.* Chet Morton had often shared their exciting adventures, but he preferred the enjoyment of a good meal to such strenuous activity.

"Tr-train robbers! I'd rather dig," Chet retorted.

He sent his long-handled shovel deep into the mire. Then, with a heave, he hoisted a load of muck and shale to the high ground behind him.

"Say, look at that shale you just tossed up!" Joe exclaimed. "It cracked open, and there are funny-looking marks inside it!"

Curious, Frank picked up a piece of the shale and inspected it more closely.

"Looks like indentations from old clamshells, doesn't it?" he remarked.

"Oh, you find all sorts of queer marks on rocks and things which have been under water," Chet answered. "That's nothing at all. Throw the silly thing away and let's get on with this job!"

Just then a voice sounded behind him. "Wait! Don't throw that away. It's valuable!"

Turning, the three boys discovered Thomas

"Wait! Don't throw that away!"

"Cap" Bailey, popular track coach and science teacher at Bayport High, standing on the rim of the excavation. He was not much older than his students, who held the twenty-five-year-old instructor in high regard.

"That's a brachiopod!" he exclaimed, examining the piece of shale.

"A w-who?" Chet stuttered.

"It's a valuable fossil—maybe millions of years old," Cap said with a smile. "They turn up every now and then in different corners of the world, and scientists use them to trace the development of man and animals through the ages."

Crouching down, he showed them what a perfect specimen the brachiopod was.

"You ought to take this to the Bayport Museum, Chet. I doubt that there's one like it in their collection."

Then Cap spoke directly to the Hardys. "How would you fellows like to combine some detective work with fossils?"

"I knew it!" Chet moaned. "Here goes our pool. It'll never be finished now."

Frank and Joe eagerly questioned the science teacher for more details.

"A week before school closed," he said, "I received a letter from an aunt who lives out West. Her husband, Alexander Bailey, died recently, just when he was on the verge of an important discovery."

"Was he a scientist, too?" Joe inquired.

"Yes, a geologist. It seems that about a year ago he uncovered part of what appeared to be the giant fossil of a prehistoric camel that once roamed the western United States. Soon after his discovery, one of those terrific western storms hit the spot and completely obliterated all of his work. Then he was taken ill and never recovered."

"Too bad," Frank murmured.

Chet asked how Cap's aunt expected him to find the camel since all trace of his uncle's work was lost in the storm.

"I haven't told you all the story," Cap replied. "Before he died, my uncle scratched out a rough map of the section, with the location of his original discovery indicated on it. It's a place called Wildcat Swamp."

That was all Chet needed. "Wildcats!" he exclaimed. "They're dangerous!"

"Probably it's called Wildcat Swamp," Cap Bailey went on, "because not far from the site of his discovery he had found a sign reading: 'Here lie the bodies of twenty wildcat.' "

"That's strange," Joe remarked. "Their killer must have been a mighty hunter."

Bailey nodded, "I guess anyone going into the area would have to keep his eyes open. And, incidentally, I've already found out there is some danger to even starting for the spot."

"What do you mean?" the boys chorused.

"Well, after school closed I started for Wildcat Swamp alone, in my car. Any number of people must have heard me talking about what I intended to do. I hadn't driven far when I was held up by two masked men and all my money was stolen. I was told to go back home and stay there."

"You think they meant to discourage you from going after the fossil?" Frank asked.

"Of course I'm not positive, because they didn't mention the fossil, and didn't take the map. That might have been because another car came along and scared them away. But they seemed to know who I was, and mentioned that it would be healthier for me in the East than out West."

"It does sound as if they wanted you to give up that trip," Joe commented. "But why? They sound more like thugs than scientists."

Cap Bailey nodded soberly. "The reason I came out to see you Hardys is this: How would you like to make the trip with me? I think you could be a big help. What do you say?"

"It sounds wonderful to me," shouted impulsive Joe. "How soon do we leave?"

Frank was just as enthusiastic as his brother, but more realistic in his approach.

"Three of us together should certainly be able to handle more trouble than one man alone, but first we'll have to get Dad's and Mother's okay."

As it turned out, that was no problem at all.

When they reached home, their quiet, pretty mother said she would leave the decision to their father. After the situation had been explained to him that evening, the tall, well-built detective said:

"I think such a trip would be a good experience for you boys, and besides, it might even work in with the case I asked you to help on."

"You mean the train robbers? How?" Frank asked.

"I had my operative Sam Radley tailing a fellow named Gerald Flint after he was released from Delmore Prison. Once Sam overheard Flint use a phrase that sounded like 'twenty wildcat' in such a way that he's sure it has some special significance. And now Flint has disappeared."

"Wow!" Joe cried out. "You don't mean he's in Wildcat Swamp?"

"I wouldn't go that far," his father answered. "But a good detective never misses a clue. If you boys can find out more about the 'twenty wildcat,' it may help me."

Cap Bailey was pleased to hear that Frank and Joe could go with him.

"I'll give you a couple of days to pack up," he told them.

Next morning Frank and Joe went to see Warden Duckworth at Delmore Prison. Their father had suggested that perhaps they could find out something about Flint's associates in jail. The officer was a friend of Mr. Hardy and he gladly spent some time telling the boys about Gerald Flint, an old-timer with a long record. Flint was described as a tall, loudmouthed man, who could be soft-spoken and persuasive when he wanted to be.

"Here's his picture," the warden said, and handed them a photograph.

"His best friends at our prison," the warden went on, "were Willie the Penman and Jesse Turk. Willie's a short, wiry fellow with a high-pitched voice, and one of the most cunning forgers in the country. He was released at the same time as Flint."

"What about the other fellow—Turk?"

"Jesse is still here. He's a mountain of a man—a former locomotive engineer, and an expert electrician, but not popular. He has a mean look about him—always frowning at something."

Frank and Joe were just bidding the warden good-by when they heard a clanging, followed by the deafening roar of a siren.

"There's been a break!" Duckworth shouted.

Seconds later, the ringing of the telephone added to the din. Duckworth grabbed the phone. Frank and Joe could hear excited chatter on the other end of the line. The warden turned to the boys, his eyes wide.

"It's Turk—he's escaped!"

CHAPTER II

Escape by Train

His face grim, Warden Duckworth ordered his car, then dashed from the office.

"Come on, Frank!" Joe urged, starting down the long, low-ceilinged corridor after the warden.

"I wonder how Turk got out!" Frank cried.

Reaching the outer prison yard, they saw guards everywhere, on the alert with rifles in case more of the prisoners should try to make a break.

"I was told," Duckworth said to the man at the gate, "that Turk may have escaped by jumping into a butcher's truck as it left the prison. Did you see which way it headed?"

"Yes, sir. North on Route 403. It was a National Meat truck."

Three emergency trucks came roaring up, followed by the warden's car. As the Hardys climbed in, Duckworth advised them to remain at the prison, but they assured him that they would keep out of harm's way.

At his direction, the trucks split up to comb the countryside. Other armed guards tramped on foot in search of the fugitive, while the motor crews toured the nearby roads.

"Follow 403," Duckworth told his driver.

The road passed through a wooded section, and the tires of the warden's car squealed as it took the curves at almost full speed.

"Do you think the truck driver planned this with Turk?" Frank asked.

"I'm not sure," the warden replied. "Usually an escape involves more than one prisoner. I'd be more inclined to think—"

"Look!" Joe cried. "There's a delivery truck— It's a National Meat truck!"

"You boys stay below windshield level," Duckworth ordered. "I'm going to force him to stop."

With a burst of speed they raced past the truck, sounding the siren. The driver slowed and came to a stop.

Warden Duckworth jumped out, gun in hand.

When the driver saw the gun, his jaw fell. "What's the big idea?" he shouted.

"You may be carrying an escaped prisoner!"

The driver went white as the warden approached the rear doors of his truck and flung them open.

"If Turk was ever in here, he's gone now," Duckworth said disappointedly. "I'll radio the other men."

Frank and Joe got out and spoke to the driver. "Do you mind if we have a look inside your truck?"

"Go ahead."

Climbing into the cool interior, the boys began examining it carefully for clues.

"Here's something!" cried Frank as he picked up a small wooden box. "It looks like a homemade radio."

It proved to be a miniature receiving set, so small that it fit snugly in the palm of Frank's hand. As he turned a knob, the gadget began to sputter.

"Repeating, Turk," it announced. "Freight delayed. Hook 138576 at three Rock Spring."

The voice broke off.

"That was Flint's voice," said the warden, who had just jumped into the truck.

"But what did all the gibberish mean?" queried Joe. "Was Flint in on Turk's escape?"

"Might have been," Duckworth retorted tersely. "Turk worked in the electrician's shop in the prison. He may have rigged up this communications system as part of a planned break."

"So when Flint and Willie the Penman got out they could tip him off on how to get away," Joe suggested.

" 'Freight delayed. Hook 138576 at three Rock Spring,' " Frank repeated. "Sounds as if a railroad freight may be part of the plan. You said Turk

was a locomotive engineer at one time, didn't
you?"

"That's right!"

"Three Rock Spring might mean time and
place. It's almost three o'clock now—and Rock
Spring isn't far from here!"

"Let's get moving. Rock Spring in a big hurry!"
Duckworth shouted to his police driver, and they
piled into the car. One of the warden's men stayed
behind to query the truck driver further.

"There's a water tower on the line at Rock
Spring," Joe recalled. "But the road doesn't go in
that far, Warden."

"We'll have to make the last half mile on foot."

Reaching the end of the bumpy road, they all
jumped out of the car and headed for the rail line.
Frank and Joe, still in good condition from track
work during the spring, soon outdistanced the
others. But before they reached the right-of-way
they could hear the rumble of a freight train.

"Maybe we're too late," Frank said, puffing.
"Hey! Here comes a car numbered 138576! I'll
bet that's what the message meant!"

Before Joe could answer, the car had passed
them. Suddenly the sliding door of the boxcar
opened. Then, as car 138576 moved still farther
ahead of the boys, a large hook was extended from
the interior.

"Look, Frank!" Joe shouted. "That man!"

Out of the bushes alongside the right-of-way

dashed a burly figure. Timing his sprint perfectly, he halted just as the hook reached him. With a desperate grab he caught it, and was immediately drawn inside the car. The freight thundered on.

"That must have been Turk!" Frank exclaimed.

By the time the Hardys reached the rails, the caboose had rolled by. There was no trainman in sight to hear their shouts or see their frantic signals.

Minutes later, Warden Duckworth and the driver caught up with them. Frank explained the strange getaway of the fugitive they believed to be Turk.

"I'll phone from my car," the warden said, "and have the freight stopped and searched."

He phoned the prison and instructed the telephone operator to relay the message to the railroad authorities. Then they drove back and waited in his office for word. When the report came, it was discouraging. The railroad police had opened car 138576 ten miles ahead, but had found it empty.

"Turk and his buddy inside may have seen you boys. They must have left the train somewhere along the stretch between where Turk got aboard and the next town. But we'll catch him. Prisoners don't break out of here and stay out—very long!"

The Hardys remained in the warden's office for a while, hoping that there would be further news of the fugitive. None was forthcoming except that the driver of the National Meat truck was cleared. Finally they agreed that they should get home as quickly as possible and tell Mr. Hardy of Turk's escape.

"This convinces me that Flint is up to his old tricks again," Mr. Hardy said. "There has been a series of freight-train robberies throughout the country, and it's up to me to figure out how to put a stop to them."

"Who engaged you, Dad?" Joe asked.

"The North American Railroad League, a group of railroad executives. They've been losing a lot of property in train robberies, and believing that the thefts were the acts of a single gang, they think I can break up the racket."

Mr. Hardy then went on to explain that the robbers, so far as he had been able to find out, had used either of two methods in their plan of operation.

"Sometimes," he said, "they throw up a roadblock at a strategic point, where the engineer can't see it in time to stop his train. In this way they create a wreck and make their haul during the confusion.

"At other times they manage to send false messages by radio, and induce the train crew to switch certain boxcars to specified lonely sidings. Then they move in and loot them."

"Sounds like a pretty slick outfit," Joe remarked.

"Yes. That's what makes them so tough to handle," his father affirmed.

"Dad," Joe asked, "do you suppose the phrase 'twenty wildcat' is some kind of password?"

Frank, who had been listening quietly, offered an additional idea. "It's possible that the railroad thieves have some kind of headquarters near where Cap's uncle was digging for fossils. Maybe a cache where they hide their loot."

"That would certainly account for their not wanting any strangers in that immediate area," Mr. Hardy agreed. "They may have been trying to discourage Bailey by holding him up on that first trip. As a matter of fact, they probably planned to steal the map his uncle left."

The Hardys spent another half-hour discussing the case, then the boys' father said he must get some papers ready for a plane trip to New York.

"I'm getting the eleven-o'clock flight, so I'll be there first thing in the morning for a conference with the League officials," he explained.

After Fenton Hardy had taken a taxi to the airport, the boys discussed their own trip, and the clothes and equipment they ought to take.

"I suppose we'll be on horseback a lot of the time," Frank remarked.

It was almost midnight before the brothers had

their gear packed. They were about to go to bed when the shrill ring of the telephone disturbed the quiet of the big frame house.

Frank answered the call. A woman's voice, edged with hysteria, said, "This is Mrs. Bailey, Frank. I've already called the police, but I think you should know what has happened here."

"What, Mrs. Bailey?"

"Two masked men broke into our house and ransacked it. They attacked my husband and left him unconscious!"

CHAPTER III

A Hazardous Take-off

In less than five minutes Frank and Joe were in their convertible, speeding toward Cap Bailey's home.

"I hope Cap's not badly hurt," Frank said worriedly.

By the time they reached the Bailey house, the police had already arrived. Frank and Joe dashed up the steps and were immediately recognized by the officer on duty at the door.

"Might have known you fellows would be on hand sooner or later," he said with a grin. "Where's your dad tonight?"

Explaining that Mr. Hardy was on his way to New York, Frank asked about Cap Bailey's condition.

"Nothing serious," the policeman assured the boys, and motioned them inside the house.

Cap was sitting on the sofa, holding his head,

Mrs. Bailey beside him. A police sergeant was conducting the investigation, and Cap told him the details. He was glad to see the Hardys, and after a few words with them continued his account.

"My wife and I had just returned from a concert, and I had gone upstairs," he reported, "when I heard her cry out. I found her struggling as she was being tied up by one of the masked men. The other held a gun on me and told me to stand with my face against the wall. A moment later I felt a blow on my head, and that's all I know."

His wife took up the story. "After that they turned the house upside down, searching for something. They must have been at it almost an hour. Cap was just beginning to stir again when they finally left, and I managed to struggle free."

The police officer questioned Cap. "Have you looked over your things to see if anything is missing?"

"Yes, but nothing much is gone. Only a duplicate map I'd been making for a trip I plan to take this summer, but it wasn't complete."

Frank and Joe exchanged knowing glances. The map of Wildcat Swamp!

"They didn't get the original?"

"No, I had that well hidden. You see, Officer, it's a map of a property out West that may have some value to it." With the promise that nothing would be made public, he told the sergeant the background of the situation.

Meanwhile, a policeman had been searching the entire house for clues. Now he came up to his superior.

"Sergeant, we may be able to get some prints off that back kitchen window. It looks smudgy—unless the marks were made by one of the family."

"No, I washed every downstairs window today," Mrs. Bailey asserted.

Hopefully, the police lifted all the prints they could find, and then left the house. The Hardys' offer to remain overnight, in the event that the housebreakers might return, was welcomed by Mrs. Bailey, even though Cap thought it unnecessary. The boys, after calling home to let their mother know where they were, took turns sleeping, but the thieves did not reappear.

At breakfast Frank and Joe questioned the science teacher closely as to how many people might be aware of his intended trip.

"As I told you, it was no secret at all," he replied. "Matter of fact, a reporter from the *Bayport Times* got wind of it and came around for an interview. He wrote a long article for the paper."

"Good night!" Joe cried. "Did he mention the location of Wildcat Swamp?"

"No, I didn't tell him that. But I did mention the sign that my uncle had found, and the words 'Here lie the bodies of twenty wildcat.' "

Their conversation was interrupted by the telephone. Cap answered it, and came back looking pleased.

"The police were able to trace those fingerprints—some character named Willie the Penman."

Frank and Joe almost shouted. "Willie the Penman!"

"He's that friend of Flint and Turk!" Frank exclaimed. "Now we know there's some kind of connection between Cap's mission and Dad's case!"

They told Cap and his wife about the series of train robberies which Mr. Hardy had been engaged to investigate, and also about the prison break.

"I wonder if Willie or someone else in the gang happened to see that story," Joe ruminated.

"It certainly begins to sound as if Wildcat Swamp might be a hideout, with Turk joining Flint and Willie the Penman," Frank observed.

"I take it you fellows are still interested in making the trip?" Cap asked with a grin.

"More so than ever," Frank said quickly. "The—"

"All I ask," Mrs. Bailey interrupted with a worried glance at her husband, "is that you take care of yourselves. I'm afraid that these men are desperate characters."

Joe suggested they make the trip by plane instead of by car. "We could even set out for a fake destination, to throw those guys off the trail in case they try to follow us," he proposed.

Cap and Frank weighed the suggestion and found it thoroughly practical. It would be faster and would lessen the opportunity for interference.

"Green Sand Lake might be the ideal destination to announce," Cap remarked. "It's well known as a searching area for fossil deposits, and it's only about three hundred miles from Bayport."

From there, they could go by rail to a place closer to Wildcat Swamp, procure mounts, and make the final stage by horseback. But this phase of the journey they hoped to keep secret.

Breakfast over, Frank and Joe went off to arrange details. First they contacted Jack Wayne, a private pilot who had become Mr. Hardy's right-hand man on charter flights. Jack was delighted to accept the assignment, especially when the boys outlined the reasons for the secrecy of the trip.

At home, though, they ran into trouble. During the boys' brief absence, their Aunt Gertrude, who lived with them, had returned from a visit and had taken over on the home front. An elder sister of Mr. Hardy, the energetic woman had a determined air and an eye that missed little, yet the boys were very fond of her and liked to tease her.

"Going away again, I hear," she said as the young detectives were stacking their gear in the downstairs hallway. "Fingerprint sets, radio sending-and-receiving set. Where to?"

Patiently but hurriedly they told her of having been asked to act as bodyguards and detectives for their science teacher, Cap Bailey.

"Bodyguards!" Miss Hardy gasped. "Aren't they the ones who always get shot first when someone is going to be assassinated?"

"Don't worry about us, Aunty," Joe said, grinning. "We'll duck between the bullets. And we need the radio so we can keep in communication with the undertakers just before the assassination."

Take-off was set for early the next morning. Though the Hardys were at the flying field long before the time of departure, Chet Morton was there ahead of them, greeting Jack Wayne and bringing the travelers a box of candy as a parting gift.

"It's only what I would like someone to bring me," he remarked when they thanked him.

"Let's open it right now," Joe said with a laugh. "Help yourself."

Chet casually removed as many as one hand would hold. "If you fellows need any help out West, just call on me. Well, I'd better hurry home to work on the swimming pool. So long."

He drove off and the three climbed into the cabin of the low-winged silver plane. Jack turned the switch and pressed the starter button.

Frank and Joe had flown with Jack Wayne many times before. They admired the way he handled his plane *Skyhappy Sal*.

After warming the engine for take-off, he swung the ship into the wind and lined up on the north-south runway, which paralleled the entrance road.

"All set?"

The passengers nodded, and Jack shoved the throttle forward. The powerful engine roared, and the plane rolled ahead. As it gained speed, the runway flashing below its windows, the plane suddenly gave a lurch.

Jack yanked the throttle back and the engine's roar died. But the plane's speed was still high as he eased in the brakes. The next instant a heavy jolt shook *Skyhappy Sal*. Frank, sitting on the left, saw something dart from beneath the wing on his side and bound away.

A wheel!

It rolled into the entrance road, just missing a car and causing it to swerve dangerously.

In the cockpit Jack Wayne fought to keep his careening aircraft from reaching the road. Desperately he threw all his weight on the right brake. There was a loud, grating splatter as dirt flew up over the windshield.

CHAPTER IV

Fingerprint Tip

JACK's passengers clung desperately to their seats as the tilted plane spun and skidded through the soft earth. Inches from the busy roadway it came to a halt. There was a moment of silence.

"Great work, Jack!" Frank found his voice.

Joe added his praise as Cap slapped the pilot on the shoulder. Only Jack Wayne's skill had kept the plane from turning over.

"This is a tough accident," Cap said. "How did it happen?"

"The retaining collar slipped off," Jack replied, after examining the landing gear. "But I can't understand why. A cotter pin holds the collar tight and that keeps the wheel on the axle. I checked the plane this morning. There wasn't anything wrong with that wheel!"

Frank, Joe, and Cap looked at one another, the same question in each one's mind. Had someone tampered with the plane because of them?

"Jack, would it be hard for a person to loosen one of these wheels?" Frank asked.

"Any good mechanic would know how," the pilot answered. "Why?"

Frank told him of the attack on Cap. It was entirely possible that someone had taken this method of trying to stop the trio from making the trip.

A determined gleam came into Jack Wayne's eyes. "I'll get another plane. I'm sure that the airport manager will let me borrow his. We shan't be delayed more than fifteen minutes."

Upon hearing of their plight, the manager readily offered the use of his private plane. The travelers transferred their equipment at once.

This time the plane rolled smoothly down the runway, rose, and headed for Green Sand Lake.

The Hardys admired the unlimited view below. Joe noticed another plane, a mere dot on the horizon behind them. Ten minutes later the plane was still there, exactly the same distance away.

"Frank, do you think that pilot could be following us?" he asked.

Frank scanned the horizon to their rear.

"What's the matter, boys?" Cap asked.

Joe explained, then told Jack. "How about slowing down and letting him pass?" he suggested. "Maybe we can identify him."

Jack throttled back but so did the pursuer, remaining far to the rear. All the boys could discern was that the plane was a low-winged, single-engine type similar to their own.

Soon Jack Wayne eased off his power and slanted down for a flawless landing at the small Green Sand Airport. The plane behind them made no attempt to land, and continued on its course.

"Guess we were mistaken about that fellow," Cap observed as they unloaded the baggage. A few minutes later the pilot wished his passengers good luck and started back for Bayport.

Green Sand Airport was a desolate spot in rough country several miles from town. It boasted one large frame building, which was a combination hangar and administration shack.

"I'll try to arrange for transportation to the fossil area," Bailey said.

He walked into the building, leaving the Hardys in charge of the luggage. A few seconds later Frank, peering upward, said:

"Here comes a plane. It looks like the one that was following us."

The trim, low-winged craft droned around the field, making its traffic pattern, and floated in to a fast landing.

The pilot taxied in front of the boys, whirling his ship around and blasting them with a dusty slipstream. He cut the switch, and without so much as a nod, walked off to the hangar.

The stranger was a tall man with smooth black hair. But his eyebrows were surprisingly light, which made his eyes seem like black marbles. His nose looked like a bony blade stuck on his thin face.

"Don't like him," Frank said crisply. "Did you notice his walk?"

"Queer," Joe agreed. "He slithers like a snake. I wonder who he is."

"You couldn't find out from his plane," Frank observed, walking closer to it. "The identification numbers are practically weathered off."

"Or rubbed off on purpose," Joe remarked. "And, say, look at that little insignia on the cowling."

"A snake," Frank whispered. "A snake eating a bird! It fits the fellow all right."

A fuel truck rolled toward them. As it drew closer, the boys discovered that the beak-nosed pilot was riding with the driver. He alighted and strode up to the Hardys.

"What's the idea of snooping around my ship?"

"We were just looking it over," Frank said casually. "We wondered how you can fly without license numbers."

"That's none of your business!" the man snapped. "It's due for a new paint job at the end of this run, since you're so worried about it. Now I'll thank you to move on."

He turned to the gas-truck driver. "Get me a taxi," he said.

The driver nodded, completed his refueling job, and rode off with the pilot. At the same moment Cap Bailey pulled up in an old-fashioned rented car, and the boys put the luggage on its roof. Then they set off for the fossil area. Twenty minutes later they reached the famous spot.

"The sand really has a greenish look," Frank observed.

Cap smiled. "You'll find that the study of fossils is pretty interesting. Paleontologists who dig for them are the detectives of the past, and fossils are their clues. You can tell from them what the climate was and if the place where they lie buried was dry land or ocean. The land we're standing on was once deep beneath the sea."

"This far inland?" Joe asked.

"Even farther. This green sand was left behind by an immense sea that covered the eastern part of the country many centuries after brachiopods became extinct. By the way, this sand is very good fertilizer."

"Like cheese, eh? When it's green, it's ripe!" Joe quipped.

The conversation turned to more serious matters. Cap asked the boys if they felt sure they had eluded any pursuers interested in stealing his map of Wildcat Swamp.

"I don't trust that pilot who flew in right after we did," Frank answered.

"Since we seem to be watched," Joe said, "maybe we ought to rig up a booby trap."

"What kind?" Cap asked.

"Well, if I were after any papers of yours, I'd figure they were in that brief case you carry. Let's take out what's important and leave the case in the car. Then we can walk out into the dry lake, circle around, and watch."

"And in case someone takes that brief case, how about a little of this powder?" Frank suggested as he opened one of the bags and took out a plastic vial.

"What is it?" Bailey asked.

"A special dye powder. We'll sprinkle it lightly over your brief case. It's the same color as the leather, but if anyone gets it on his hands, a blue stain will show up in a few minutes. And he'll have a terrible time washing it off."

"We may not catch the villain red-handed, but we'll sure catch him blue-handed." Joe chuckled.

The trap was laid quickly and the car parked in plain sight. The three worked their way across the dry lake bed, around boulders, and through scraggly stunted brush toward the top of a hill.

But before they could reach the summit, a voice hailed them, "Hey there! What are you up to?"

Cap and the Hardys stopped in their tracks and

turned. A uniformed policeman had dismounted from a horse and was hurrying toward them.

"I've been watching you," the officer puffed. "You don't act like fossil hunters to me. I patrol this area every day—lots of professor guys get lost out here—but you're not fossil men. You don't even have any equipment."

Cap told the policeman of the trap they had just laid and why. "Will you help us?" the teacher asked.

The policeman became interested. "Hm! Sounds exciting, and nothing exciting ever happens out here. My inspection's over. I'll go along with you."

He plodded behind the others up the low hill and crouched with them in a clump of thick brush.

Joe whispered excitedly after a few minutes, "Look!"

There was a movement in the weeds near the car. Suddenly two men stood upright and glanced about furtively. Then, swiftly and silently, they moved to the car and opened a rear door.

CHAPTER V

Into Perilous Country

"DON'T jump them yet!" Cap Bailey hissed at Frank and Joe as they crept toward the car. "Let those thieves commit themselves!"

The two men snooped around inside for a moment or two. Then one of them picked up the brief case and began to paw through its contents.

"Now!" yelled Cap, and the Hardys and the police officer sprinted from cover.

Although both invaders were big, the policeman's gun held them at bay.

"What were you fellows looking for?" Cap demanded.

"Nothing," the larger man muttered.

"W-we're just hungry and thought there might be some food in this car," the other said.

"Looks to me like you had a pretty good idea of what you wanted," the policeman said sharply. "And it wasn't food."

"I'm sure you're right," Frank agreed. "Can we get these fellows into custody around here?"

The officer produced two sets of handcuffs from his saddlebag. Then he asked Joe to ride his horse and ordered the two snoopers into the back of the car. He sat between them with his gun out and ready for action.

The jail was five miles away, but it did not take long for them to cover this distance, even proceeding at a pace slow enough for Joe to canter along behind. Reaching the small wooden structure which served as town hall and jail, they all went inside.

"We didn't do anything. You can't hold us!" the big man protested when they were arraigned before the local magistrate.

"Names, please," the magistrate ordered.

"Uh—Jake Johnson."

"Jim Jones. How long you gonna hold us?"

Frank and Joe pulled Cap into a huddle a short distance away.

"Listen, Cap, the thinner chap looks just like a picture that Warden Duckworth showed us of Gerald Flint," Frank whispered.

"And the other guy sure fits the description of Jesse Turk," added Joe.

Cap considered. "We don't want to let them know we suspect their identity. How about getting fingerprints from Warden Duckworth?"

The trio called the magistrate aside, explaining their suspicions and the necessity for concealing their identity.

"I can't hold them without a warrant," the official told them.

"We can prove enough now to give you cause to hold them until the prints arrive," Frank said.

Going over to the huge man, he asked him to hold out his hands. Unsuspectingly, the man complied.

"You see that blue stain on his hands?" Frank asked the magistrate. "That came off the brief case belonging to our friend. I dusted the case with a special chemical powder before we left the car. It's proof this man was handling it."

Snarling like trapped animals, the suspects were led away to cells in the rear of the building.

Frank put in a long-distance call to Bayport. Fenton Hardy, delighted that his sons had outwitted the men, promised to have the warden send the fingerprints to the Green Sand authorities.

"Now for Wildcat Swamp!" Joe said elatedly as they left the jail.

"Let's see. From here we can get a train as far as Red Butte," Cap remarked. "We'll arrive there in the morning, and get our horses and supplies."

They enjoyed a good meal in the train's dining car and discussed plans for suitable equipment. It was still early morning when they arrived at their destination, and Cap thought they had better use the hotel as a temporary headquarters. He led the way to Red Butte's only hostelry, the Silver Saddle.

"Breakfast for three, hey?" the bewhiskered clerk greeted them. Learning they had just come from Green Sand, he said, "Have ye heerd the big news up there? It was on the radio early this mornin'."

Frank nudged Joe, smiling, and Cap grinned too.

"Couple o' guys broke outta that there jail," the old man went on.

Frank's head came up with a start, and Joe and Cap snapped to attention immediately.

"Did you say someone got away?" Joe demanded.

"Two fellas, just stuck in there yestiddy for stealin' outta someone's car, busted clear out last night. Got clean away!"

The three travelers looked at one another gravely. Turk and Flint—if it had been they—were on the loose again!

After some deliberation, the trio decided to leave as soon as possible for Wildcat Swamp.

"While we're waiting for breakfast, I'll send a message to Dad," Frank said. "He ought to be kept informed of what's going on. Suppose you two buy camp provisions while I contact him."

"Okay," Joe and Cap replied.

Frank hooked up the powerful little radio set. Switching to the secret frequency used by the Hardys, he called his home.

Fenton Hardy was disturbed when he heard of the desperadoes' escape. He agreed that there was nothing for the boys to do but to proceed to the swamp as planned.

As soon as Joe and Cap returned to the hotel with their purchases, they all sat down to breakfast. Then the three went out to buy the digging implements they would need. At the general store the obliging clerk said:

"Since you're heading into dangerous country, I'd advise you to take along pistols. Only last week a trapper shot an ugly wildcat out there."

"Thanks for the tip," Joe answered. "Do we need permits?"

"Not for pistols carried in plain sight."

"Then we'll buy three."

At the livery stable to which the clerk directed them, they were able to hire three sturdy saddle horses and a strong pack mule.

By midmorning they had packed their camping gear onto the mule and were ready to start off. Cap and Joe took the lead, with Frank bringing up the rear holding the animal's rope.

"Wildcats, here we come!" Joe cheered as they cantered from the main street of Red Butte and headed for the desolate-looking country southwest of the town.

"According to Uncle Alex's map, it's a good twenty-five miles to the swamp," Cap called to the boys. "And this is pretty rugged country!"

The trail followed a swift little stream that wound back and forth through the uneven, rocky ground. The sun became scorching hot.

"We won't reach the first landmark until some time tomorrow morning," Cap commented when they stopped for lunch. "That will be a big tree near the ridge of a small mountain."

"Any kind of a decent-sized tree would look good to me," Joe said, perspiration soaking his shirt.

"You sure get tired of looking at this brush, and sand, and rocks," Frank agreed.

By late afternoon the extremely slow, steady plodding had brought them to a more fertile area, with scattered trees and lush grass. The long trek had taken its toll of riders and horses. All were tired, irritable, and jumpy.

"Listen to those coyotes howl," Joe muttered. "They're the spooks of the prairie, all right."

"We'd better not go more than a couple of miles farther before we bed down for the night," Cap advised. "Once the sun sets here, it gets dark fast." A short while later he called a halt.

Cap busied himself getting the sleeping bags unpacked and feeding the animals. Frank and Joe soon had a simple supper ready. After eating, Frank led the horses to the stream which had been their guide all day, and let them drink all they wanted. Then, after tethering them, he stepped back into the little circle of light made by the rekindled campfire.

"All set for the night," he announced. "Hope it doesn't rain."

"Not much chance," Cap predicted. "Look at those stars. You certainly don't see them that bright back in the city, do you?"

"Almost bright enough to travel by," Frank remarked. "But say, what's that light off there to the left?"

All three stood up and studied the distant glow.

"Someone else is camping out here," Frank decided. "Maybe Flint and Turk."

Joe, impulsive as ever, cried, "Let's ride over!"

It took only a few moments to bank their fire and saddle the horses.

Keeping well apart and permitting their mounts to pick their way in the darkness, the trio moved toward the light.

"It's a campfire, all right," said Joe. "Look!"

He was the first to spot the men crouched around the small blaze. "There must be half a dozen—and horses, too."

His mount had discovered the presence of other horses, and now let out a loud whinny. Immediately excitement broke out around the campfire. The men scrambled to their feet, ran to their horses, mounted them, and rode away quickly.

The young detectives wanted to follow them, but Cap insisted that it would be unwise since they themselves were not familiar with the territory. They carefully inspected the camp for clues but found none other than the hoofprints.

"Did you notice that one of the riders went off alone?" Joe asked. "I wonder why. The rest of them beat it in the opposite direction."

"Here are the marks of his horse," Frank said, turning his flashlight on the ground. "Small hoofprints, too, as if it were only a pony and probably carrying a very light rider. I—"

"Are you thinking what I'm thinking?" Joe interrupted. "Willie the Penman?"

"Could be," Frank replied. "And say, the prints lead in the direction of Wildcat Swamp!"

"You're right!"

"We can't be too careful the rest of our trip," Cap warned as they made their way back to their own campsite. Nothing had been disturbed, and despite their curiosity about the mysterious riders the three soon dropped off to sleep.

Joe was first to awake the next morning, and whipped up a solid breakfast before rousing the others. They paid a brief visit to the mystery camp before setting out for Wildcat Swamp, but gleaned no further information.

"After we cover the next mile or so we ought to start looking for that big tree on the map," Cap

Six outlaws were crouched around the campfire

spoke up. Since early morning the three had come quite a distance from the camp on the plain.

They were in hill country now. The trail wound through rugged terrain with patches of woodland. They rode along the rim of one small canyon and through the dry bed of another. After considerable time had gone by, Cap said:

"I certainly expected to see that big tree by this time. If Uncle Alex was right, we should be in sight of it, and there's nothing here but this scrubby pine."

"There's no sign of a big tree but that old stump by the edge of that ravine," Frank said, pointing.

Joe jumped off his horse to examine it, while Frank and Cap checked the map.

They were interrupted by a shout from Joe. "Come here! This isn't an old stump. The tree has just recently been cut down!"

When the others reached him, Joe was scraping away at the top of the stump.

"Look! This has been covered with mud to make it look like an old cut." He pointed.

"But where's the tree?" Cap demanded.

Frank looked over the edge of the ravine. "Down there," he announced.

"The tree was felled within the last couple of days, maybe only yesterday," Cap observed.

"By the men we saw at the campfire last night," Frank conjectured.

"How about the map that was stolen from you back in Bayport—the unfinished copy? Had you put the tree on that?" Joe asked Cap.

"Yes. It was one of the details."

Frank stared at the teacher. "Then I'm sure, Cap, this was an attempt to remove a landmark we've been counting on to help us find Wildcat Swamp."

The trio pushed on, stopping only a short time to rest their horses and eat lunch.

As they rode through the heat of the afternoon, Cap asked the boys if they had noticed the formations that looked like giant toadstools made of clay and sandstone.

"Yes," Frank answered. "I was wondering what keeps them from crumbling."

"It's the sandstone overhang which prevents the clay column from eroding," Cap told him. "Back in the glacier age, they were separate deposits, and all the clay except that protected by the sandstone has eroded."

The cavalcade skirted the edge of a deep ravine, the trail following a bench that dipped gradually toward a stream below and ended in a narrow grassy shelf.

Permitting the horses to drink and to graze on the scanty grass, the riders dismounted to stretch their legs.

Suddenly Joe's voice rang out in alarm. "Frank! Look out!"

But his warning was too late. Before Frank could even get his arms up to defend himself, a tawny streak of fur and muscle launched itself through the air from the rocky ledge above.

It was an enormous wildcat!

CHAPTER VI

Deadly Danger

THE big cat was in midair before Frank was even aware of it. He had no time to defend himself.

As the beast leaped at the boy, his horse instinctively reared and screamed. The action distracted the cat and gave Frank time to recoil a step, so that the animal missed its target.

Crack!

A sharp explosion came from behind, and the wildcat sank to the ground. Another quick report, and the snarling, spitting beast lay lifeless.

Frank turned and saw Joe, his gun still smoking, looking coolly at the still form of the wildcat.

Cap broke into a relieved chuckle and remarked, "I certainly knew what I was doing when I picked you boys as bodyguards!"

After making sure his attacker was dead, Frank pushed the carcass over the cliff. Then they took up the trail again.

"This is the longest twenty-five miles I've ever

ridden," Joe remarked after a while. "I feel as if I've been in the saddle a month."

Cap admitted that they had made slow progress, but he felt that they had done well enough considering the difficulties of the trail. Late in the afternoon they came to a spot where he suggested they make camp. In the morning, the ride toward Wildcat Swamp was resumed with renewed zest.

"The next, and last landmark on the map," Cap stated, "is a big needle rock with a balancing boulder on top. It's on a ledge, halfway down from an overhanging cliff to a long, sandy slope that ends in the swamp itself. The fossil should be somewhere in that sandy slope."

Leaving the stream, which whirled away in a southwesterly direction while they continued west, the fossil hunters eventually came to the entrance of a long, narrow defile.

"We must be getting close!" Cap said excitedly. "The map shows this gap leads to the ledge above the needle rock."

He went ahead through the passageway, with Frank following and Joe trailing with the mule.

"Here we are!" Cap exclaimed as he came out of the dark, shadowy defile onto a wide ledge.

A moment later the boys joined him on the ledge. To their right was a sheer cliff wall rising to a wide plateau.

To their left, the ledge fell away in a sloping, sandy decline, while straight ahead, at a turn in the ledge, stood the towering rocky column on which rested a huge, heavy boulder.

"Look at the size of that boulder!" murmured Joe in amazement. "It's so delicately balanced it looks as if I could push it off."

"You might be able to at that," Cap agreed as he studied the phenomenon.

"Look at that wooded mountain beyond the swamp," Joe said. "There's a fire tower at the top."

Just then Cap raised his hand for silence.

"Listen!"

From the plateau above them came the sounds of a familiar, steady drumming. Hoofbeats!

"Let's go!" Frank cried, spurring his horse back through the defile.

With Joe and Cap close behind, it was only a matter of minutes before he burst out through the dark ravine to the open terrain.

Just ahead of them was a single horse and rider. With a swoop, the trio surrounded him. To their surprise, the newcomer proved to be a young boy.

"Hi, there!" Frank greeted the youngster, who looked to be about fourteen years old and handled a horse as if he had been born to the saddle.

"Hi," the boy returned. "Who are you?"

Cap Bailey explained that they were scientists, looking for fossils.

"This is my mother's property," stated the youngster. "Who said you could dig here?"

"Oh, then your mother must be Mrs. Sanderson!" Cap recalled that his aunt had stated in one of her letters that Mrs. Sanderson had given her approval of the exploration.

"That's right. I'm Harry Sanderson."

Cap introduced himself and the Hardys, and told Harry why they were there. He added that they would pay for the right to hunt fossils.

"Oh, no, you won't have to do that," Harry assured him. "Mr. Alex Bailey, when he first talked to my mother, promised that she would get all the money any fossils might bring."

"We'll go along on the same promise," Cap assured the boy.

"We liked Mr. Bailey," Harry remarked. "He seemed to be a nice man, but a short while after he settled things with my mother, he disappeared. We heard later that he got sick and died."

"We hope to finish the job he started," Cap told him.

Frank and Joe cautiously questioned the boy, asking who lived in the area.

Harry smiled. "Nobody but us and the sheriff. Lately, though, I've seen campfires and strange men. The other night a couple of 'em stopped me and started asking a lot of questions. But I slapped my horse and got away."

"What did the men look like?" Joe asked.

"Both of 'em were big, but one was the biggest guy I ever saw! Bet he could be a wrestler if he wanted to. The other man looked like he might be a lawyer or a doctor. He talked in a low voice."

Frank and Joe looked at each other and knew what the other was thinking. The descriptions fitted Turk and Flint!

"If those big hombres stop me again," Harry said stoutly, "I'll get the Forest Rangers after 'em."

"Oh, there are Forest Rangers in this section?" Joe asked.

"Sure thing. They make regular visits through here, and they always stop at our ranch."

"Is that the fire tower they use?" Frank asked, pointing to the top of the mountain rising beyond the swamp.

"No. That old one's been abandoned. There's a new tower you can't see from here."

"That's good to know," Cap commented.

"Yes, and Sheriff Paul's ranch isn't far from us, either. He's a good friend, too."

"Say, Harry, you must know this territory pretty well," Frank said. "Are we right in thinking that's Wildcat Swamp down there?"

"Wildcat Swamp? Never heard it called that, or any other swamp around here."

"Are you sure?" Cap was plainly upset by this revelation.

"That's Devil's Swamp down there," Harry said.

Cap and the Hardys looked at one another in

dismay. Could they be off the track in spite of the map which they had followed so closely?

"Well, I have to get along home," Harry said. "Hope you'll all ride over to our ranch sometime. My mother'd like to meet you."

"How do we get there?" Frank inquired.

Harry pointed in a northwesterly direction. "There's a trail along the left side of that mountain."

He slapped his pinto and was off across the plateau in a cloud of dust.

"So this is Devil's Swamp and not Wildcat Swamp," Joe said in disgust. "We come over a thousand miles by plane and train and—"

"Wait a minute," Cap interrupted. "I'm going to check this map again."

For several minutes he studied the map in silence, then a smile of understanding slowly broke over his face.

"This has to be the place," he insisted. "There couldn't be two such spots so much alike. Uncle Alex probably named it Wildcat Swamp on his own, not knowing what the local people called it."

"There's one way to make certain," Frank remarked. "That's to find the sign about the twenty wildcat."

"If it's still here," Cap said hopefully. "Anyway, let's pick out a place to make camp. Then we can look around."

After scanning the territory they agreed upon a

wooded section of the plateau just above the mouth of the defile. All three occupied themselves with unpacking their gear and setting up the tent.

Cap and Frank found some suitable stones for a fireplace, and laid a small grate across the top. This done, the boys were eager to start exploring.

"Don't do any wandering around here without wearing your high boots," Cap warned. "No telling what you'll run into down at the swamp."

Frank dug out the three pairs of thick wading boots which they had purchased in Red Butte and they all donned them, along with sturdy corduroy breeches. Light jackets would suffice, they decided, because the sun was still high in the sky.

Cap, still sure that this was the right spot and eager to see if there were any signs of his uncle's work, told the boys to go ahead. They pigeon-toed their way down the sandy slope to the edge of the green marsh.

"What a mixture of growth!" Joe marveled at the lush, odorous tangle as Frank led the way into the swamp, keeping to the high hummocks and leaping over the black, watery, evil-looking expanses that spread everywhere.

"It's amazing," observed Joe, "how we passed through such a barren region only a few miles away and wind up in a water-logged spot like this!"

"Cap said that's the way this section of the country is—all extremes," Frank said.

Excitedly Joe grabbed his brother's arm. "There it is! The old sign!"

Nailed to a shaggy willow tree, almost completely enveloped with vines that grew up its trunk and wound around its branches, was an old, weather-beaten board. The Hardys cleared five feet of muck and landed next to the tree.

"This is it! *Here lie the bodies of twenty wildcat'*!" Joe read.

They hurried back to camp. Cap was delighted to hear that the boys had found the sign. "From now on I can see that we're in for some plain, old-fashioned hard work with pick and shovel."

The trio unpacked digging tools, and then headed back to the spot on the slope which Cap had selected.

Swinging the heavy picks, they soon loosened the top layer of sandy soil. But then the harder work began.

"This is really packed down," Frank grunted as he swung the pick into hardpan and penetrated only a few inches.

They had worked for an hour when Cap unearthed an old tin can. He was about to throw it away when he took a second look and let out a yell.

"Bonny Briar smoking tobacco! That's the kind my uncle used to smoke."

"Then we're working in the right place!" Frank exulted. "Unless," he amended, "some other guy was around here who smokes the same brand."

Cap refused to be talked out of his belief and dug with renewed energy. It was only a few minutes later when Joe's pick hit into the dirt with an odd ringing sound.

"Ouch!" he howled, wringing his hands as he dropped the wooden handle hurriedly. "I could feel that shock all the way up to my elbows!"

"What did you hit?" Cap queried.

"I don't know, but it sent a vibration right up the handle of this pick."

More careful this time, Joe probed in the same spot, and gradually scraped dirt away from what appeared to be a length of metal.

As he worked, it became apparent that the object was heavy, rusted piping. Finally he uncovered its entire length.

"How in creation did that get in here?" Frank asked, turning to Cap.

The young man was completely stumped. "Uncle Alex wouldn't have used piping," he mused. "And to the best of his knowledge, there had never been any previous exploration here."

They were still studying their unexpected discovery when high above them they heard a great thud and a rumble. Frank, first to look up, gave a shout.

"The boulder! It's toppled off the column! Here it comes!"

With a roar the great stone gathered momentum, sending smaller stones scurrying to all sides, then hurtling down the incline, straight to where the three were digging!

"Look out!" Joe screamed, jumping as far to one side as he could. Frank was already in midair, leaping to the other side.

With a crash the boulder tore across their excavation, pulling what seemed to be half the hillside with it, and thundered into the swamp with a tremendous splash.

Thankful to be alive, Frank and Joe gazed at each other, then looked for their companion.

But Cap Bailey was nowhere in sight!

CHAPTER VII

Skeletons and Schemes

"CAP! Cap Bailey!"

There was no answer to the Hardys' frantic calls. Following the thunder of the crashing boulder, the stillness was frightening.

"Quick! We'd better clear away some of this rubble!" Frank ordered.

Rocks and shale of all sizes and shapes had broken loose in the landslide. Sand had been scooped from one spot and piled high in another. Desperately the boys rooted through the debris.

"Joe! It can't be! Cap just couldn't be—"

"Frank! Down there! Something's moving!"

They tore wildly at the rubble until they had cleared Cap's face and shoulders. Groggy, the teacher drew in great lungfuls of air, until they pulled him free.

Finally he was able to sit up and move his arms and legs to show that he was unharmed.

"Boulder . . . must . . . have . . . been . . . tipped," he said huskily. "Go . . . see . . ."

Frank and Joe rushed up the slope but could find no trace of any person on the ledge. A quick glance revealed no one near the rock column from which the boulder had become dislodged.

"Let's take a look on the plateau," Joe said, and they hurried along through the defile.

Atop the flat ground, they saw nothing at first that could be connected with the fall of the boulder. Then off toward the trail around the left side of the mountain, Frank's keen eyes spotted a cloud of dust.

"Two riders!" he shouted.

The Hardys knew they could not hope to overtake the men.

"Anyhow, we've got to get back to Cap," said Joe.

When they reached the rock ledge, the boys could see that Cap felt considerably better. As they skidded down the incline toward him, he gestured excitedly.

"Look at this!" he exclaimed, and pointed to a large object he had picked out of the debris.

Frank and Joe examined it curiously. "What is it?" Frank asked.

Cap spoke triumphantly. "Unless I'm very much mistaken, it's a bone from the leg of an ancient horse. It was turned up by the boulder when it ripped down the hill."

"An ancient horse? You mean that there were prehistoric horses in this country?" Joe asked.

"I thought the horse was a comparatively recent animal," Frank chimed in.

"Oh, no, the horse has been part of the earth as far back as man can tell. As a matter of fact, the evolution of the horse is one of the interesting mysteries of paleontology."

"What do you mean—mystery?"

"No one has figured out why the horse—a much smaller one than the present kind—lived here from prehistoric time until the Pleistocene period, then became extinct. The horse as we know it today was imported."

"If this fossil is from one of the earlier breed," Frank observed, "it must be mighty valuable."

Bailey nodded. "If I'm right, it could mean there may be many valuable fossils here besides the prehistoric camel my uncle discovered."

Cap was so excited that all thoughts of his brush with death were forgotten. When the boys told him of the two riders they had seen in the distance, he merely nodded.

"If they did tip the boulder, actually they did us a favor. Look at the digging they saved us."

"But if they continue to make attempts on our lives," Frank said, "we'll have to be on guard every second."

"Is there any possibility of getting help in this excavation job?" asked Joe.

Cap shook his head impatiently. Elated by the discovery of the fossil, he was ready to start work immediately.

"If those men were trying to stop us by toppling the boulder, they probably think we're dead, and won't be coming back," he added.

Frank and Joe, eager themselves to see what other fossils might be turned up, fell to work in earnest.

For several hours they sweated as they dug deeper into the sand and hardpan.

"I've hit something!" Frank suddenly called out. When it was uncovered, Cap Bailey was enthusiastic.

"Boys, I'd bet my last shirt that this bone was once part of the shoulder structure of the ancient camel Uncle Alex thought he'd found!"

"Looks like an oversize ham bone that some prehistoric dog buried here," Joe said wryly. He sat down in the sand and propped his weary head on one grimy fist. "You really have to be interested in fossils to work this hard," he groaned. "I'll never think of geologists and scientists again as old fuddy-duddies."

Cap and Frank burst into laughter.

"Better buck up, Joe, we've barely started." Cap clapped him on the back and asked him to carry the ancient bones up to their permanent camp, and to put the fossils under a protective tarpaulin.

"What are we bothering to cover these things for?" Joe queried. "Nobody's been taking very good care of them for a couple of million years."

"Except nature," Cap said. "She's been protecting them from the weather all this time."

Joe nodded and set off across the slippery sand and through the defile.

Cap and Frank picked up their shovels and resumed work, chopping out large chunks of near-petrified sand. The pit grew deeper and deeper. They were working in silence, intent upon the task at hand, when Frank began to feel uneasy.

Where was Joe? He had been gone much too long for a mere trip to camp. Frank climbed out of the excavation and scanned the slope. He could not see his brother.

Worried, Frank hurried toward the plateau. Had something happened to Joe?

Sensing trouble, Cap followed Frank, reaching the camp a few minutes later.

"Joe doesn't answer," Frank said. "But," he added, pointing to a tarpaulin wrap, "there are the fossils. He's been here."

"How about the horses?" Cap asked, and quickly investigated the tiny meadow where they had tethered the animals. All three horses and the pack mule were grazing contentedly.

"I'll try our distress signal." Frank gave a long, piercing birdlike whistle. It was the secret whistle he and Joe used when in trouble.

But no answer came, and again Frank gave the shrill, high-pitched call. Listening intently after it ended, all he and Cap could hear was the breeze as it gently moved a few leaves high above them.

"But what could have happened to Joe?" Cap asked. "If he met with any sort of trouble, we should have heard some kind of sound."

After discussing the situation, they decided on a systematic search of every foot of ground between the camp and the slope. They had got as far as the ledge when Cap held up a warning hand.

"Do you hear something?"

For a moment there was only silence. Then, almost as if from under their feet, in the depths of the earth, they heard:

"Frank! Fra-a-a-a-nk!"

The voice was so low and indistinct that Frank thought he might have imagined it. But a look at Cap's excited face convinced him that his companion had heard the call too.

Where was it coming from?

After several minutes of frenzied search they had the answer. A flash of light from between two huge rocks just below them at the very edge of the slope caught Frank's eye.

"Down there!" he cried excitedly.

He and Cap peered into the crevice. This time a light shone squarely in their eyes, and they realized that they were staring into the beam of a flashlight.

"Hey! Come on down!" It was Joe's muffled voice. "It's a cave, and somebody's here!"

Examining the opening, Frank and Cap realized that a man could easily squeeze through it. Rigging a stout rope around a large boulder as a means of ensuring their exit, they wriggled down the rope and into the passageway. In a minute Frank stood beside Joe on the floor of a sizable cavern.

"You're okay? You didn't have an accident?" Frank asked.

"Not exactly," Joe answered. "I tripped, fell off the ledge, and rolled down here. When I saw this cave, I thought I'd investigate—and look!"

He pointed with his flashlight to one of the recesses of the cave. Propped against the sloping wall was a skeleton!

"Nice cave mates you pick for yourself, Joe!" Frank said jokingly. He spoke lightly, but a shiver ran down his back as he gazed at the skull.

"Listen, fellows, that man probably died from suffocation or starvation in here," Cap said. "I wonder whether he had been living in the cave."

"Anyway, he had plenty of equipment with him," Joe said. "See?" His flashlight picked out a pile of long, rusty iron pipes near the skeleton.

"Say, they're the same kind as the pipe you found on the slope, Joe!" Frank cried. "This old geezer must have brought them down here for a purpose."

"He probably was a prospector," Cap decided. "I wonder what he planned to do—drain the swamp?"

"But what for?" Joe asked.

"Maybe he had panned some of the slope," Frank said, "and believed it might be a good prospect for placer mining."

All three joined in rummaging around the cave with their flashlights. Cap was about to suggest that they return to the surface, when Frank excitedly cried out:

"Come here, quick!"

Hurrying over, they found him in a dark corner. He had spotted a gleaming new pistol.

"Someone else has been here, and not long ago," he announced. "There's not a speck of rust on this gun."

Carefully Frank wrapped a handkerchief around the weapon and picked it up. By the beam of his flashlight, they all could clearly see the smudges of someone's hand along the barrel.

"I have that fingerprint powder in my pocket, I think," Joe said. "Let's see what those prints look like."

He dusted the smudges, and Frank examined the clear prints. There was a familiar swirl on one that looked like a thumbprint.

"Doesn't that remind you of the thumbprint of a certain character named Willie the Penman?" Frank asked excitedly.

"It sure does—on the kitchen window of Cap's house," Joe replied.

"If so, what's our next move?" Cap asked.

"To prove our point," Frank replied.

He proposed that they leave the pistol in the cave, on the chance that the owner would return, and they could capture him then.

"We can watch from above," the young sleuth suggested.

"Good idea," Joe said, and Cap agreed.

Making sure they had left no telltale traces of their presence, they climbed up the rope through the cleft in the rocks to the ledge above.

All agreed that further digging for fossils must wait upon this new development. There was a good chance that the owner of the pistol had been watching them.

Evening chores were split up among them. Cap hid the precious relics, while Frank prepared supper, and Joe watched the cave entrance from a spot in the shadows. The trio ate supper in Joe's hideout.

"We'd better stay right here tonight," Cap proposed.

By dusk the three watchers were ensconced in a makeshift shelter. Lying prone, they could see every bit of the slope around the entrance to the cavern. A full moon provided all the illumination needed.

"We'd better agree on shifts," Cap suggested,

and it was decided that Frank would have the first watch. Joe would take over at midnight, and Cap at three in the morning.

There were no disturbances during the night and at six o'clock Cap awoke both his companions.

"I was sure somebody'd come back for that pistol," Joe said, disappointment in his voice. "Well, I'm going down to have another look in the cave."

"I'll go with you." Frank crossed the slope with his brother and descended to the floor of the cave. A moment later the boys looked at each other in astonishment.

"The pistol's gone!" they cried simultaneously.

"But how could anyone have taken it?" Joe demanded. "Not a soul came near the cave."

"Unless," Frank said, "there is another entrance."

It took only five minutes for the boys to investigate Frank's theory. After probing every niche and cranny of the walls, he found a loose boulder which looked as if it had been set in one corner for a purpose. Moving it a bit, Frank saw daylight.

"Come on," Frank motioned, and the boys crawled through.

They found themselves farther along the slope, around the corner from the spot where they had lain watching all night!

"What a couple of duds we turned out to be," Frank said in disgust. "And what a laugh Willie or whoever it was had on us!"

"I wonder if he saw us lying there in wait," Joe pondered.

Replacing the stone that covered the entrance, they called to Cap and showed him the second underground entrance. The teacher's reaction was almost identical with Frank's, and he added, "This place may be riddled with secret caves, and eventually bullets, if we don't watch out."

A short conference produced one decision—to radio Fenton Hardy and tell him that Willie the Penman might be in the neighborhood of Wildcat Swamp.

Frank unpacked the powerful sending-and-receiving equipment. They surveyed the terrain for a good working spot.

"Below this mountain ridge, we'll certainly have trouble getting a good signal," he murmured, and decided that the only possible way to make contact would be to use the self-inflatable balloon they had brought to carry the antenna aloft.

Soon the little gas-filled bag was high in the sky, trailing its aerial wires. Frank tuned in the secret frequency that the Hardys used for family communication. He was about to give it up as hopeless when suddenly a voice said:

"Fenton Hardy speaking. Come in! Come in!"

Quickly Frank reported that they were well, and then told his father of the latest developments.

"Will you get prints of Flint, Turk, and Willie from Warden Duckworth and send them to Red Butte as soon as possible," he requested. "We'll check them with the ones on the pistol we found last night."

His father agreed.

"How about the train robbers?" Frank asked. "Any news?"

"I have a hot lead I'd like you boys to—"

Mr. Hardy's voice faded completely. There was not a sound from the receiver.

Startled, Frank glanced toward the airborne antenna, just in time to see the balloon, deflated, plummet to the earth.

Now there was no chance to find out what the detective had intended to say!

CHAPTER VIII

Ordered Out

"WHAT happened?"

Cap's cry was hardly out of his mouth when Joe and Frank were racing off to retrieve the deflated bag. It dropped out of sight, but by following the dual cord which had secured it to the set and carried the antenna line, they soon located it. The balloon hung limply from the branches of a tall pine. Frank shinned up, unfastened the bag, and brought it below for examination.

"Punctured," he said. "Look at those holes."

Cap came running up just in time to hear Frank's remark.

"But how—so high up in the air? Nobody could throw a stone that far—not even a baseball pitcher!"

Frank's face was grave. "I believe someone fired a bullet through it."

"But I didn't hear any shot," Joe objected. "Did either of you?"

"The shot could have been fired from the other side of the ridge," Frank commented.

Cap nodded. "Especially if the wind were blowing the other way—which it is—we wouldn't have heard the shot."

"I wonder," Frank mused, "whether some cowboy took a potshot at it just for fun, or if our friend Willie did it deliberately."

"I wish we could find out just what is behind all these goings-on," Cap said. "It doesn't seem likely that a gang of ex-convicts would be worried about our finding a few fossils. What can be the real secret of Wildcat Swamp?"

"It must be pretty valuable for somebody to go to such great lengths to protect it!" Frank stated with a tight smile.

Slowly they walked back toward camp, winding the antenna wires on the spindle as they went along. Even though the balloon itself was useless now, the aerial could be salvaged.

They had almost reached the tent when they heard the sound of hoofbeats behind them, coming down the ravine. Tight-lipped, they waited for the horsemen to appear.

"Oh, it must be the Forest Rangers," Joe announced, relaxing, as three green-uniformed riders appeared.

The one in the middle was short, wiry, and

gruff-looking. To his left was a medium-sized man, and the third ranger, also short, had a peculiarly flat nose.

"Who are you birds?" asked the wiry leader.

"What are you doing in these parts?" the flat-nosed one spoke up.

Courteously, Cap introduced himself and the Hardys, explaining their business in the community.

The leader, who apparently was indifferent to the fit and condition of his uniform, nodded.

"Well, I have bad news for you. You're going to have to call it all off."

"What do you mean?" Cap demanded.

"I mean that we're ordering you to pack up your stuff and clear out of this territory."

"But we have permission from the owner!" Joe protested, stepping forward. "She knows all about this expedition!"

"I said you'll have to pack up and clear out," the spokesman retorted in a rasping voice. "If you must know, this is an order from the government."

"For us to get out?" Cap asked unbelievingly.

"Everyone around here has been ordered to move all belongings away," the ranger continued. "It's going to become a government reserve."

In dismay, Cap and the Hardy boys looked at one another. If the government had closed the territory, there was no alternative for them but to leave. Cap begged for an extension of time, but was turned down.

"Get on the trail," the ranger ordered.

He and the other men followed the fossil hunters to their camp and stood by to see that they packed up. Discouraged, the three went through the process of folding the tent and dismantling all their permanent fixtures.

"Get a move on! We haven't got all day!" the leader of the rangers commanded, watching the proceedings with a grim smile.

"All right, but we have to pack some of this stuff carefully," Frank answered as he began to stow away the radio equipment.

"Say, son, have you got a state license for that?" the officer asked. "If you haven't we'll just have to take it."

Frank was astounded. "State license? I never heard of such a thing. I have my regular radio license."

"That's not enough. You need a special one around here," the spokesman announced. "Short wave, ain't it? Yep, that's the story. Pick it up, men," he ordered the other rangers.

"But you can't do that!" Joe sputtered. "The radio belongs to us."

"Sure, sure, and you can have it back," the man replied, "by calling at our district office for it next month."

Despite more protests, the rangers, fingering their holsters, coolly appropriated the set. Discouraged and quiet, the trio rode off toward Red Butte, with the three men in uniform following them to see that they left the area.

Cap was downhearted because he had come close to finishing his uncle's task. Although he had the two pieces of fossil carefully stowed aboard the pack mule, he was sure other parts of the ancient camel remained on the slope. What a thrill it would have been to find a whole skeleton!

"All right now, just keep going a good ten miles before you stop," called the leader of the rangers. "And after this, do your fossil digging some place else besides Wildcat Swamp!"

There were no words spoken among the three as they jogged along. But as soon as they had put sufficient distance between themselves and the rangers, they halted and held a council of war. It was decided not to put more than a mile between their new camp and the swamp.

"I'm not going to leave here until this whole mystery is solved," Frank said determinedly. "Government reserve or not, if Willie and Turk and Flint have anything to do with this place, I'm going to find out about it."

"Me, too," Joe added. "I never thought of it, but we probably should have told the rangers our suspicions."

"After we compare the fingerprints from the pistol with those your father's sending," Cap spoke up, "we'll have more to go on."

They dropped off the trail and dismounted near a small brook. Doggedly they went about the business of establishing their new base in a well-concealed spot.

"Dad said he'd send the prints by air mail," Frank commented. "They'll probably be in Red Butte before we can get there ourselves."

Cap looked at the Hardys more spiritedly than any time since they had been ordered away from the region of the swamp.

"Say, it might be a good idea if I started tonight for Red Butte," he said. "Then I'd get there just in time to pick up the letter, and could head back here as soon as I had it. Traveling by moonlight ought to be safer than in broad daylight, the way things are going."

Much as they disliked seeing Cap go off alone, the boys had to agree that his idea made sense.

"In the meantime, we can guard the gear and keep our eyes open for those jailbirds," Frank said.

After a quick supper they helped Cap saddle up, and made sure he had enough provisions to last the trip. After he had ridden off, the boys, deciding against a campfire, crawled into their sleeping bags and lay down.

"I certainly didn't think much of those

rangers," Joe remarked with a yawn. "I always thought that rangers were well-uniformed, neat, and trim. That little mangy guy in the middle was the sloppiest-looking ranger I ever saw."

"Say, I've been thinking about that very thing," Frank retorted. "A lot of things those rangers said just didn't ring true—like that license business about the radio."

"They sure were nasty and I've always heard that rangers are polite," Joe said, recalling particularly their leader's parting shot. " 'Do your fossil digging some place else besides Wildcat Swamp,' " the boy repeated in a voice imitating that of the ranger.

Frank suddenly sat up. "Joe! Do you realize what that ranger said? *Wildcat Swamp!*"

"Sure. What about it?"

"Don't you remember Harry Sanderson telling us it's called Devil's Swamp?"

Joe's eyes grew round as he realized the implication. "Local rangers would probably have called it that, too."

"Exactly. Those men might be phonies. Let's get back to the slope and see what's going on!"

Quietly they rode through the brush, keeping off the trail as much as possible, until they were less than half a mile from the upper mouth of the defile. There they tied their horses, and went on afoot.

Down the defile they crept, listening for alien

sounds. In a short time they were standing on the rock ledge above the slope. The moon had been blotted out by a cloud a moment before, so now there was blackness all around them.

Joe grabbed Frank's arm. "Look down there!"

Shining from the entrance to the cave was a bright light!

CHAPTER IX

Lost!

"LET's crawl down and look in the cave!" Joe whispered.

"Okay. But take it easy. There may be a guard, and when that cloud passes over, we'll be good targets for him."

Stealthily the Hardys crept down the incline. It was treacherous going in the darkness, without the rope, and complete quiet was absolutely necessary.

"Can you see anything?" Joe whispered as they finally reached the lip of the opening and Frank peered cautiously over it.

The answer was a tightening of Frank's grip on his arm. Wriggling closer, Joe's eyes searched downward into the cavern, and he nearly cried out.

Below them were the three rangers!

The boys could hear the murmur of their voices

but could not make out their muffled conversation.

Unable to determine exactly what the men were doing, Joe tried to squirm around for a better view.

On the very edge of the opening, his elbow slipped. Before he could prevent it, a stream of pebbles and stones cascaded down into the cave!

"What's that?" grunted one of the men.

The boys heard startled exclamations as the rangers in the cave jumped to their feet.

"Someone's up there! Get 'em!"

Furious that they had been discovered, the Hardys scrambled up the slope. There was no use trying to be quiet now, and they slipped and stumbled as they made their way toward the ledge.

Behind them, there was an uproar as the rangers gave chase. Just then the moon came out from behind a dark cloud and the ledge was bathed in moonlight.

"Run faster!" urged Frank as they headed for the shadows of the defile.

There was hardly need for Frank's advice. Joe already was tearing along at top speed. Just as they reached the entrance of the rocky passageway, there was a loud report behind them. *Pt-s-s-s-ee-ee!*

A bullet whistled overhead, then another, and another. The sound of flying lead lent wings to the feet of the Hardy boys.

The sound of flying lead lent wings to the Hardys

"Stay off the trail! Cut across the other way!" Frank hissed.

Joe let his brother pass him. Frank dashed through a tangle of underbrush, up the steep slope of the defile, and into the woods. They struggled over rough ground, running into low-hanging branches, tripping over roots, falling to hands and knees innumerable times.

A wild search was made with flashlights by the rangers behind them. Again and again the boys dodged the beams. Finally they were able to throw off their pursuers, and they breathed a sigh of relief when all sounds of the chase ceased.

Frank and Joe stopped to rest. After a breathless moment, Joe found his voice to express new concern.

"What if they find our horses!"

"Just hope that they don't. Anyway, we're safe! I wonder where we are. I've lost my bearings completely."

For some time they searched in vain in the darkness for a familiar landmark, but in the shadowy woods there was little they could see. Joe was about to suggest that they give up looking for camp until morning, when Frank whispered:

"SSS-s-st! A light!"

Up ahead, they could see a dim light bobbing in midair, as if it were suspended from nothing.

A few seconds later there came the soft clop-

clop of a horse's hoofs slowly picking a path among the trees.

"Maybe the rider's meeting someone here," Joe said.

Quickly the Hardys found cover, and waited. Within minutes the rider came abreast of their hiding place. The soft glow of the lantern he held lit up his youthful features.

Harry Sanderson!

"Golly, are we glad to see you!" Joe greeted him. "We're lost."

"I'm just as glad to see you!" the boys replied. "I was on my way to find you."

Frank explained what had happened, from the time they had been ordered out of the fossil area to the present moment. When he heard their description of the rangers, Harry said he did not know the men. And oddly enough, he had never seen the cave.

"You didn't tell us Wildcat Swamp was to become a government reserve," Joe chided him.

Harry's eyes flicked wide open in amazement. "It's not true. I mean, my mother and I haven't heard anything about it. Something mighty funny's going on. A man came to our ranch this evening to buy the swamp."

Harry went on to say that a stranger had dropped in with papers to show his mother that Devil's Swamp and a lot of the ranch belonged to someone else, and the man was going to buy it from the real owner.

Frank and Joe were baffled by Harry's revelations. They began to realize that a great deal was happening in the Wildcat Swamp area that was mysterious and which their father would want them to investigate.

"All my mother really owns," Harry went on, "is the house and a few acres around it—at least that's what the man said."

"Who was this man?" Frank asked, his eyes flashing with indignation.

"His name is George Moffet. I never saw him before. Guess he doesn't live around here. He was a little guy, pale and beady-eyed."

"Willie the Penman, I'll bet!" Joe exclaimed.

"Willie who?" Harry asked.

Without telling him that Willie was an ex-convict, Joe said he had acquired the name because he could imitate other people's signatures.

"If your caller was Willie, he probably drew up the papers himself," Frank said. "Harry, you tell your mother not to give up any papers and not to sign any unless we see them first. She shouldn't even show her deed to this impostor. Keep it locked up in a safe place. Hurry!"

"Thanks a lot, fellows," Harry said. "I knew you'd help me." He said good-by and rode off.

The Hardys continued their search for their

horses. They found the animals safe. Apparently the rangers had departed.

Quickly the boys leaped into their saddles and reached the camp without further adventures.

To their relief, nothing had been disturbed, and once more they crawled into their sleeping bags. Next morning Frank and Joe discussed the strange events of the previous evening.

"Doesn't it strike you as strange that three new rangers were sent here in addition to the others already located in this area?" Joe asked Frank.

His brother nodded. "And it's not natural for men in that position to be whispering in a cave. I'd like to sneak back to the swamp in daylight and see what's going on."

"Go ahead. I'll watch camp. We can't take a chance on having our stuff stolen."

As soon as they had eaten, Frank went off to reconnoiter. His careful approach through the defile and the ledge was effort wasted, he discovered. There appeared to be no one around, and no trace whatever of the men who had been there only a few hours before.

Without Joe to stand guard for him outside, Frank did not attempt to enter the cave. But he played his flashlight into both entrances and satisfied himself that they were vacant. The only explanation he could think of was that the rangers might comprise a special group to evacuate people from the new government reserve. If the Sanderson ranch actually was to be turned into a reserve!

Back at camp, he said to Joe, "As soon as Cap gets back I think we can take a chance digging again. As long as we don't carry away any fossils, there won't be any harm in looking for them."

Joe agreed. In the meantime, he wanted to keep busy.

"I think one of us had better get in touch with Mrs. Sanderson," he said. "Harry may have been stopped before reaching home."

"I'll stand guard here this time," Frank said. "You ride over to the ranch."

With Harry's directions to guide him, Joe started out for the Sanderson ranch house. The path led over fairly rough country on the other side of Wildcat Swamp. Joe saw no evidence of grazing cattle, though there were occasional grassy stretches that would have afforded pasturage. He scared up several rabbits, and took a potshot at a fox about to devour one.

Presently the way led up through another rocky defile, similar to the one near camp. Joe was halfway through this narrow ravine when he heard the sound of horse's hoofs from up ahead. The horseman was coming straight in his direction and there was no place to hide from a possible enemy.

The strange rider bore down on him from around a curve in the trail. Twenty paces ahead the newcomer's horse shied, stumbled over a loose stone, and threw his rider headlong.

Like a sack of meal, the rider struck the ground and lay still.

"This can't be a trick," Joe thought to himself. "He hit the earth too hard!"

Cautiously, nonetheless, Joe dismounted and approached the fallen rider, who had not moved.

Joe took hold of him, turning the rider over on his back.

It was Chet Morton!

CHAPTER X

Three Odd Letters

"CHET! Chet Morton!" Joe shouted in disbelief.

His friend did not stir. Joe flipped the top of his canteen and held the cool water to Chet's lips. The boy moaned and tried to rise.

"Joe! No, it couldn't be. I guess I'm dreaming. I'm still kayoed."

"You're not dreaming, Chet. What are you doing way out here?"

Chet rested several seconds before replying.

"Morton's Pony Express. Modern variety," he said cheerfully. "Boy, that spill knocked the wind out of me. I have a message for you guys. Several, in fact."

"Is Dad okay?" Joe asked apprehensively.

"Oh, sure. Your dad and I flew to Red Butte together yesterday afternoon with Jack Wayne."

"You and Dad?"

"Yeah. He's hot on the trail, I guess. Those train robbers are going to the hoosegow."

"Well, what's the news?" Joe asked eagerly.

"I have the fingerprint pictures you asked for," Chet said as he struggled awkwardly into his saddle.

"Come on, Chet," Joe said. "I'll show you the way back to camp and while I'm there I'll compare those prints with the ones we found on the pistol."

As they rode along, Chet told Joe the reason for his sudden trip to the West.

"Your dad thought I'd enjoy it," he began. "And also, he didn't trust anyone else to give you an important message. He thought Sheriff Paul probably would know where you were, so just before he took the midnight train, he told me to contact the sheriff and have him take me to Wildcat Swamp."

"Where did Dad go?"

"He was as secretive as usual," Chet said.

"Did Sheriff Paul bring you?"

"No, he wasn't at his office, so I rode out to his ranch. But he wasn't there either. Nobody was."

"Then how did you find this place?" Joe asked.

"A nice kid reined up in front of the Paul ranch just as I was about to leave," Chet said. "Name of Harry Sanderson."

"We know him."

"Yeah, he told me you did, and he showed me how to get here. Knows all the short cuts. And boy, he can ride like the wind!"

Chet paused for breath, then asked, "How's Cap?"

"All right, I hope. He went to Red Butte. Funny you didn't see him at the hotel."

"He wasn't registered."

This turn of events worried Joe. Had Cap been attacked on the way to town?

"Nothing seems to be turning out right on this expedition," he told Chet, and brought him up to date on all that had happened.

"At least you now have a copy of the fingerprints you wanted," Chet remarked with pride.

Arriving at camp, Joe flung himself from the saddle. "Hi, Frank!" he yelled. "Look what I found along the trail."

"Chet! How'd you get here? You look as if you'd ridden all the way from Bayport."

"I had a spill," Chet confessed. Then, repeating his mission, he pulled a packet from his jeans and handed it to Frank.

Eagerly Frank tore it open. It contained magnified copies of three sets of fingerprints—Turk's, Willie's, and Gerald Flint's. The Hardys at once compared them with those taken from the pistol.

"Look at this whorl," Joe cried excitedly. "No mistaking it. The gun we found in the cave was once in the hands of Willie the Penman. And I'll bet it's in his shoulder holster right now!"

Chet let out a whistle. "He's—he's after you guys?"

"Guess he is," Frank said.

"In that case"—Chet gulped—"I'd better get back to Bayport and finish digging our swimming pool."

"Before you eat?" Joe needled him.

Chet grinned. "I'll stay till morning. Got to get some rest, anyway."

"Hold it!" Joe said suddenly. "Did you give us all of Dad's messages?"

"Hey, it's good you reminded me," Chet answered. "I forgot something."

"What?"

"Your dad wants to see you."

"When?"

Chet pushed his Stetson back and scratched his head. "Let's see. Just before midnight on the seventeenth."

"Where?" Frank asked impatiently.

"On the railroad siding near Spur Gulch." Chet pulled a map from his pocket and handed it over.

"Frank, that's real news from Dad!" Joe exclaimed. "Something's doing. A trap for the train robbers, or I miss my guess."

"Could be," Frank said. "I hope we can clear up some of the mystery around here before we leave to meet Dad in two days. I think we ought to find Sheriff Paul and tell him about Willie the Penman. And we still have to see Mrs. Sanderson."

During the evening the boys waited expectantly for Cap, hoping someone in town had told him of Chet's arrival. But Cap did not come.

"I'm afraid he never reached Red Butte," Frank said fearfully. "And now that we know Willie the Penman is in the neighborhood, I'm worried."

With concern on his face, Chet pulled a bright bandanna from his pocket and mopped his brow.

"Honest, fellows, I have to start back for Bayport in the morning."

"But as long as you are here, wouldn't you like to help us dig up a camel?" Joe suggested.

"A what?"

"That's right. We've found one."

Chet began to weaken. "Well, I might stay a day or two."

When morning came and Cap still had not appeared, the Hardys decided that one of them should go to Red Butte to investigate.

"I'll go," Chet said. "As long as you guys need help, I'll stick around for a while."

He mounted his horse like a bear cub trying to straddle a split-rail fence. After he had ridden off, Frank and Joe saddled their mounts for the ride to Sheriff Paul's ranch. They hid their camping equipment in a rocky depression, covering it with brushwood, then set out.

It was quite a long ride to the ranch, but finally they reached it. Picketing their horses, they knocked on the back door, which immediately was opened by a trim, middle-aged woman. When the boys introduced themselves, she asked them in.

"We have a few worries we'd like to talk over with the sheriff," Joe said.

"My husband isn't here," Mrs. Paul replied. "And I have a few worries too. He hasn't been home for three days."

"Three days? Is that unusual?" Frank asked.

"He got a phone call and told me there was trouble about some rangers. I didn't get the details, because he rode off in a great hurry."

Joe gave his brother a sidelong look. Rangers! Could it be the same three men who had ordered Frank, Cap, and him away from the swamp? Frank caught his brother's glance and nodded in reply.

"I guess we'd better leave a note for the sheriff," Frank told Mrs. Paul, who promised to give it to him as soon as he returned.

"Maybe we'd better go back to where we hid our supplies and not go to the Sanderson ranch just now," Frank told Joe after they had finished the lunch graciously offered by the sheriff's wife.

The boys headed back toward camp. When they were still some distance from it, Frank, hearing voices, reined in suddenly. Dismounting, he and Joe walked forward cautiously.

"Chet! Cap!" Frank exclaimed.

Cap explained that he and Chet had met shortly after the stout boy had left for Red Butte.

Cap, having heard about Chet's arrival and departure from a restaurant owner, had started back but had lost his way.

"I—I like it better here now," Chet said. "I think I'll stay till you all go. With Cap here, there are four of us. Just let Willie the Penman dare to show up!"

The tension relieved, they all laughed and set about preparing supper.

As night fell and there still was no sign of the rangers, Frank said, "Let's sneak back and do some more digging."

Armed with flashlights and tools, the four carefully made their way down to the fossil deposit. Chet was impressed, and wanted to see more of the camel. However, he soon tired of the digging.

"What's the matter, Chet?" Joe asked. "Break your shovel?"

Chet grunted and went to work. It was becoming evident that the fossil they were excavating was an enormous one.

"I believe we have a perfect specimen," Cap said enthusiastically.

Chet found plenty of excuses to rest from his labors. Only the sarcastic remarks of his friends kept him digging in the spot designated to him. He had not been at it long when he unearthed a half-rotted board.

"Huh," he said, "all I can do is find clam fossils in Bayport and old billboards out here."

Frank looked up suddenly. "Billboards? Where?"

"Here," Chet said, beaming his light on the rotten piece of wood. "It has letters on it. E R S. What does that mean?"

"Could be part of the name Sanderson," Joe said.

"Perhaps an old prospector left it here," Cap volunteered.

Frank snapped his fingers. "I have it!" he cried. "Wait here. I'll be back in a second."

Without explaining why, he dashed off in the darkness.

"I think he ate some locoweed," Chet remarked, leaning over his shovel and heaving a sigh.

The words were hardly off his lips when a shriek of terror sounded in the night.

Was Frank in trouble?

CHAPTER XI

Underground Snare

CATAPULTING himself out of the pit, Joe dashed down the slope in the direction Frank had taken. Chet and Cap hurried after him. With their flashlights stabbing the blackness, they finally reached the edge of the swamp.

Just then a flashlight beam was turned on Joe and a familiar voice called, "What's going on? You guys sound like a stampede of water buffalo."

"Frank! Was that you who yelled?"

"No. I thought it was one of you."

"Must have been a wildcat," Cap said. "They sometimes sound like humans."

"Say, Frank, where were you going in such a rush?" Chet asked.

"To get that sign on the tree. I have an idea about it."

With the others following, he pushed through the dark swamp to the gnarled willow tree.

Frank pointed out the dangling sign to Chet. Then he yanked the weathered old board loose.

"I want to compare this with the piece of wood you found, Chet," he said.

As they struggled back up the hill to the pit, Chet puffed and heaved. "You sure—make things —hard," he said.

Joe was the first to notice that something was amiss at the pit.

"Hey! I left my shovel right here. Where'd it go?"

"Everything is gone!" cried Cap.

"The board too," Frank said. "We've been robbed!"

"That cry was just a trick to get us away from here," Cap declared. "Somebody wanted our tools. Put out your lights, boys. There's no sense making targets of ourselves."

The four stood motionless in the darkness. Frank broke the silence by whispering that it would be hopeless to try finding the thief in the darkness. The logical move was to return to their campsite as secretly as possible.

By this time all of them except Chet knew the route well enough to find it in the dark. Chet stumbled along between Frank and Joe. Reaching camp, they crawled into their sleeping bags.

"Now tell us about the sign, Frank," Chet whispered.

"I was going to try fitting the two pieces together. I think originally it was all one sign."

"But that would mean it doesn't refer to wildcats at all," Chet pointed out.

"Right! It would read, 'Here lie the bodies of twenty wildcatters'!"

"Wildcatters has two *t*'s," Joe reminded him.

"The second *t* could have been right on the break," Frank explained, "and easily have rotted away."

Chet still did not see the real significance. "What's the difference whether there were twenty wildcats or twenty wildcat hunters here?"

Cap spoke up. "A wildcatter, Chet, isn't an animal hunter. He's a man who hunts for oil-well locations."

"Oil prospectors!" Chet whistled. "You mean there might be oil here?"

Cap said that was quite possible, and then Joe exclaimed, "Those rusty pipes we found could have been part of some drilling equipment! And that skeleton in the cave might have been another one of the wildcatters!"

"Sk-skeleton!" Chet quavered.

"Oh, we didn't tell you about our Mr. Bones!" Joe laughed. "Wait till you see him. He's out of this world."

Chet crawled deeper into his sleeping bag and was silent.

"Seriously," Frank said a moment later, "I won-

'der what really happened to those wildcatters, and when."

"I've been mulling that over myself," said Cap, "and I've about decided that it couldn't have been too long ago."

"I think you're right," said Frank.

"Well, I feel we can be certain," Cap said, "that there still may be a few men living who learned about the possibility of oil below the swamp from some of those wildcatters. That's why they're trying to run us out of here."

Frank remarked that a certain George Moffet seemed to fit right into this theory. No doubt he was trying to get Mrs. Sanderson's property.

"Is there any way of telling where there might be oil except by drilling?" Chet asked Cap.

"Yes, indeed," the teacher replied. "In certain periods in prehistoric times far more oil deposits were formed than in others. If I could locate some fossils from one of those periods, I'd know we've made the right guess about the situation here. Incidentally, every big oil company today employs a paleontologist for this kind of exploration."

"If we're going to do any more digging," Chet spoke up, "we'll have to buy some more tools."

"Joe and I might get them in Red Butte after we see Dad," Frank suggested. "Tomorrow night we plan to meet him at Spur Gulch, Cap," the boy added, and told him about Chet's message.

Bailey volunteered that he and Chet buy the

tools. They would stop at the Sanderson ranch and tell Harry and his mother their suspicions.

Next morning, an hour after sunup, Frank and Joe set off in an easterly direction, while the others went northwest.

"I'd like to look around that cave once more before we leave," Cap said when they reached the ledge. "Besides examining those pipes again, we may find other clues to prove we're on the trail of the old wildcatters or of some new ones."

Chet was reluctant, but on the other hand, he didn't want the teacher to think he lacked courage.

"Okay, Cap. Lead the way!"

When they reached the narrow opening in the rocks, Chet glibly offered to remain at the cave entrance to "guard the horses." Cap grinned as he dismounted.

"If there's trouble," the teacher said, "we're better off together than split up."

"You've talked me into it," Chet replied solemnly.

Flashlight in hand, Cap stalked ahead of him down the incline to the cave entrance below the ledge. At the end of the passage, where it broadened out into the wider portion of the cave, Bailey's light flickered.

"Battery's getting low," he muttered to himself.

As Chet beamed his own light around, Cap entered the inner part of the cave. Stepping past the skeleton, barely discernible in the dim light, the teacher bent to pick up a rusted section of pipe. As he did, a faint sound in a recess of the rock wall made him straighten up.

"That you, Chet?"

"What did you say?" Chet boomed from the passageway.

In sudden alarm Bailey swung his fading flashlight toward the wall. It picked up a dark figure crouching in the gloom.

"Don't move!" came a whispered command.

At the same moment, an arm snaked around his chest like a hoop of iron, pinioning his arms to his sides. With a clatter, Cap's flashlight dropped to the rock floor.

"Chet!" he gasped. "Get help! Hurry!"

"Shut up!" his attacker hissed.

The arm tightened its grip, choking off any further warning. As Cap struggled, another man rapped him sharply on the side of the head with the butt end of his gun. The science teacher crumpled to the floor.

"That'll take care of him for a while!" the gruff voice muttered in the darkness. "Now let's get the other one."

But Chet, having heard Cap's desperate plea for help, had made his decision. Even though he was scared, Chet would never run out on a friend in distress.

He had recently learned some elementary judo.

As a flashlight suddenly beamed in the passage-way, Chet poised himself. Seconds later a man of medium height emerged from the inner cave.

As Chet had been taught, he let out a blood-curdling scream and shouted some unintelligible gibberish. His amazed adversary stopped in his tracks. The boy backed away a few inches. If he could keep this up until he reached the entrance—

The man, though, was not to be fooled a second time. He lunged savagely at Chet. Instantly Chet grabbed his outstretched arms and pulled his attacker sharply forward. Off balance, the man stumbled toward him.

With split-second timing, Chet brought his knee up sharply against the man's chin. He went down like a sack of lead sinkers.

Not knowing there was a second enemy, Chet relaxed. Suddenly his hands were locked behind him in a firm grip. He tried to break free, but the attacker twisted his arms painfully.

Resistance was futile.

CHAPTER XII

Ambush

WHILE Chet was struggling with his new enemy, the man he had knocked down began slowly to get to his feet. Holding his jaw, he shone a big flashlight on the boy and glowered.

"Wise guy, eh? Break his arm, boss."

"Can the cracks! Get on with this job!"

The injured man's companion collared Chet and shoved him deeper into the cavern, where the other fellow stuck a candle into a crevice and lighted it.

In the eerie glow Chet saw Cap lying prone on the ground. Then, for the first time, he got a good look at the second assailant, a small, wiry man wearing a badly fitting green uniform and holding a short rifle.

As Chet stared, Cap came to and staggered to his feet.

"You're the rangers who ordered us out of this area!" he charged.

"Very clever!" the scrawny man said sarcastically. "But since you weren't smart enough to take a friendly warning, we're going to teach you a lesson!"

"Listen here," Cap retorted angrily, "I demand that this boy and I be treated according to law. You have no right to hold us without valid complaint."

"No? Well, we're taking the right."

"You can't get away with this!" Chet said hotly. "We know who you are, and we know what you're after! You're impostors, and you're trying to steal Mrs. Sanderson's land!"

"And you," Cap added, pointing at the wiry man, "you're Willie the Penman!"

The other man looked startled. "They know we're—"

"Shut up!" the small fellow ordered. He turned to Cap and Chet. "You don't know what you're talking about. If you have any sense at all, you'll keep your mouths shut." He turned back to his companion. "Give me the wire."

The captives were led deeper underground, back into the dim recesses of the cave. Then the men, using lengths of tough copper wire, tied their prisoners' hands behind their backs and bound their ankles.

"Are we being kidnapped?"

The little man said with an ugly laugh," I

wouldn't call it that. We're not taking you any-
where. You're just going to lie right here in this
cave and have a good rest."

"Yeah, and when we get around to it," his
henchman added, "we'll send the sheriff to pick
you up."

With that, the two men left the cave. When the
sound of their footsteps had died away in the
gloomy vault, Chet spoke up. "Do you think they
really will send the sheriff to get us?"

"I wouldn't count on it," Cap replied. "I can't
picture those two criminals helping the law."

"Do you suppose Frank and Joe will ever find
us?" Chet quavered.

Meanwhile, the Hardys had altered their plans.
Since they did not have to meet their father until
midnight, they had decided to ride first to Sheriff
Paul's and find out about the "ranger trouble."

Upon reaching the Paul ranch, the boys dismounted and knocked on the front door. To their
amazement, it swung wide open under Frank's
touch.

Joe called out, but there was no reply. He
peered into the neat living room.

"The place is deserted and the note we left is
still on the table!"

"That's funny," Frank remarked. "Mrs. Paul
must have gone off soon after we did."

"I hope nothing's happened to her," Joe said apprehensively.

The boys circled the house, but there was no sign of the sheriff's wife. Nor was she in the barn or any of the other ranch buildings. The boys were more mystified than ever.

"Let's go back to the house," Frank suggested.

In the kitchen they saw unwashed dishes on the sink—a startling contrast to the spick-and-span condition of the house. Near the door was a basket of clothes. On a hunch, Frank felt them.

"They're still damp, Joe. That means Mrs. Paul was interrupted in her work. She must have left here in a hurry. Let's check the corral."

Joe, first to reach it, called out, "Look at these fresh hoofprints. Several riders were here."

Frank knelt down. "Three sets come up to the gate, then four go away. The question is, Did Mrs. Paul go with the others, or leave later?"

Carefully checking the trail and the turnoff into the ranch, the boys discovered that one set of hoofprints were headed in another direction.

"She might have ridden off to warn somebody about her visitors," Joe said, "probably her husband. But why didn't she use her radiotelephone? I noticed one in the living room."

Hurrying back to the house, Frank examined the set. "The sheriff no doubt uses it to contact police headquarters at Red Butte. I'll do the same."

He switched on the set and waited for it to warm up. However, no hum came from the loudspeaker. He pressed the microphone button.

"That's funny, Joe. This set doesn't seem to be putting out at all."

Frank tried again, but the output dial remained at zero. Turning off the set, Joe unsnapped the cover slides, and removed the top.

"No wonder!" he exclaimed. "A tube is missing!"

"That's proof enough for me," Frank cried. "Those visitors were here for no good reason."

"We'd better ride to Red Butte as fast as we can and report the whole situation," Frank said grimly.

"Right," Joe agreed. "Then later we can hop a train from there to Spur Gulch."

Hurrying outside, the Hardys sprang into their saddles and galloped off. At this rapid pace, they quickly covered a mile. Then they were forced to slow down because the trail had entered a rocky valley.

As they proceeded, the valley became a narrow pass walled in by steep rock formations on either side.

"I guess it'll have to be Indian file now!" Frank said, cantering in front of his brother. As they neared the end of the pass, he suddenly reined in.

"What's up?" Joe asked, almost colliding with Frank's mount.

Frank did not answer, but from up ahead, Joe heard a gruff voice shout:

"Hold it!"

A man in cowboy attire, astride a pony, blocked the exit to the pass. The boys couldn't see what he looked like, because of the dirty blue kerchief tied over the lower part of his face and a ten-gallon hat pulled low on his forehead.

"I see you're packing a gun!" he remarked, looking at the weapon Frank carried in a holster.

"Yes. Protection against wild animals."

The cowboy gave a sarcastic laugh. Then he pressed his horse up beside Frank's mount and tried to make a quick grab for the boy's gun.

But Frank was alert. As the stranger's arm shot out toward his holster, the boy stood up in his stirrups and brought his fist down hard on the man's wrist.

Frank's gun clattered to the ground. His horse reared, making the stranger's pony shy too, and the masked man lost his seat. His own weapon was dislodged and flew several feet away as he hit the sand.

"Come on, Joe!" Frank cried. "Help me tie this guy up, quick!"

As Joe slid off his mount, he grabbed the rope from the pommel of his saddle and hurried to assist his brother. It was dangerous business, maneuvering in the narrow pass among the excited, rearing animals.

Scrambling to his feet, Frank's assailant began to back out of the pass. He reached for his gun. Realizing it was gone, he turned tail and started to run.

"Help!" he shouted.

Frank and Joe ran to intercept him. Joe tackled the man about the knees and dragged him to the ground. Frank, following up his move as fast as he could, seized the man's flailing arms.

But even as he did, Frank spotted a quick flash of movement to his left.

"Watch out, Joe!" he yelled. "There are more of them!"

Two masked men now sprang forward. As the Hardys whirled to meet this new threat, the ambushers charged!

CHAPTER XIII

An Icy Dungeon

"GET 'em!"

Though completely helpless under the double-barreled Hardy attack, the mysterious enemy managed to shout orders to his oncoming aides.

Frank side-stepped a fist from one of the other masked men and landed a hard blow on the attacker's chest. As Joe ducked a charge from the third ambusher, their fallen leader arose and dived at the boy from behind.

Thrown off balance, Joe was an easy target for his two opponents and went down like a tenpin. Against three, Frank stood no chance at all, and was quickly pulled to the ground.

Within a matter of minutes, the boys were bound and gagged, then heaved crosswise onto the saddles of their horses.

"These men must be some of Willie's gang,"

thought Frank as the horse started to move. "Now what?"

There was no indication from the cowboys as to where they were taking the Hardys. Except for a terse command now and then by their leader, the men guided them silently on a grueling ride through the rough country. Two of their captors rode ahead, the other at the rear.

"Why have they kidnapped us?" Joe's mind was in a whirl. "How did they know where to wait? They must have had us under surveillance all along!"

One hour went by, two, three. Frank and Joe had been in many a tight spot, but none had ever seemed so hopeless as this one. Each jog of horse and saddle against stomach and ribs knocked the breath from their bodies. The boys realized they were becoming so exhausted and sore that even if they could manage to struggle free, they would not be able to walk.

Worst of all, they realized that they now would have no chance of meeting their father at Spur Gulch.

Hours later Frank and Joe heard the whistle of a train and shortly afterward they were approaching the railroad line. As close as Frank could figure, they were intersecting the railroad right-of-way much farther west than Spur Gulch.

From behind a massive rock beside the shimmering tracks came the sound of a horse's whinny.

The man in the lead halted. He thrust two fingers in his mouth and gave a shrill whistle. Immediately another masked man rode into view.

"So you got the meddling kids!" he boomed. "Great work! We'll get rid of 'em right away!"

"What's your plan?" asked one of the others.

"Toss 'em on the rails!"

From their awkward positions, lying across their saddles, the boys studied the newcomer. He was a big, heavy-set fellow. Could this be the convict Jesse Turk, who had so cleverly escaped from Delmore Prison?

The other man who was as tall, but not as heavy as the newcomer, shook his head. "You want us all sent up for life—just when we can get clear?" he shot back. "I've got an idea how to put these smart-alecky kids out of the way and make it look like an accident."

"How?"

"The freight that's coming through here from the west at ten-thirty is hauling refrigerator cars. It's due in an hour. We'll put these kids on ice!"

"Hey, that sounds like a good deal. I go for that." And the others readily agreed.

The heavy-set fellow spoke up again. "Break out some chow. We'll give these boys their last meal."

As Frank's and Joe's horses were led away from the main party, their guard drew a bowie knife.

"Toss 'em on the train rails!"

Dismounting, he slashed the ropes that bound Frank's wrists and ankles.

"Get off and untie your brother," he ordered roughly. "And no tricks! Hear me?"

Frank was only too glad to obey. He unfastened the handkerchief that had been stuffed into his mouth, and hobbled over to where Joe still lay across his mount. While seeming to struggle with the knotted bonds, he whispered furtively:

"Joe, I'm sure the newcomer and the other big man are the ones we captured at Green Sand Lake. Flint and Turk!"

"I think you're right. But we're not going to sit here and let them get away with this, are we?"

"I'll say not! Dad wants these crooks, and we'll get 'em. Soon as the kinks are out of us, I'll give you the signal and we'll put up a fight."

"Cut it out!" their guard shouted. "No talking!"

By the time Joe was untied, supper was brought to them by one of the masked men. Seated with a rifle across his knees, he watched the captives eat while the other guard walked off for his dinner. The boys were hungry enough for a good meal, even though their minds were occupied by the grave danger facing them.

As Joe set down the tin can from which he had been drinking water, he whispered, "Frank, how come they left only one guard over us? Where are the rest of them?"

Frank smiled grimly. "The others wanted to eat, I guess, and you can't eat with a bandanna over your mouth! They don't want us to see who they are."

Hearing their murmuring, the guard turned. "All right, you wise guys, one last warning. You want your gags back on? One more sound outta you, and—" Suddenly he stopped, cocked his head, and let out a loud roar. "Well, we don't have to worry about you much longer. Here comes the freight."

As the train drew nearer, the rest of the gang appeared and surrounded the captives.

"Get ready for your last mile," the brawny man said sardonically. "Curtains for two detectives— and one to go!"

The boys winced. By "one to go" the scoundrel could not mean anyone but their father. They must know he was in the vicinity of Spur Gulch! He might even have been captured already!

Crouching behind a low outcropping of rock along the tracks, the men forced the boys down with them. The railroad ran up a slight grade at this point, and the heavy Diesels struggled and churned as they reached the incline. Slowly the twin locomotives neared the hidden group.

"This'll be a snap," one of the men said confidently. "I'll break the seal on a cooler first, and then—"

Suddenly Frank sprang up. "At 'em, Joe!"

"Hey, what's—?"

The man's cry was cut off abruptly as Joe's fist crashed into his mouth. Blood spurted from his lips, and he gave a yell of surprise and pain.

Shoving one of their abductors backward into another and sending both sprawling, Frank turned and butted headfirst into a third.

As they battled against the heavy odds, the boys shouted at the top of their voices for help. But their cries were lost in the thunder of the Diesels as the big engines roared past. No one on the train had seen the ruckus, and now no one could hear it!

Although the Hardys fought furiously, they were outnumbered by their enemies. Subdued, they were held this time in steellike grips. The man who had proposed the refrigerator cars had ridden down the tracks, watching for a "cooler."

As one passed, he urged his horse alongside. The animal kept pace with the moving car while its rider leaned over toward the door. Skillfully he broke the metal seal and slid open one of the heavy insulated doors.

The open car drew abreast. Frank and Joe were seized tightly, then heaved up and into the yawning opening of the refrigerator car. The heavy door slammed shut, and they could hear the bar fall into place on the outside.

Joe was first to speak. "Frank! We're locked in," he said hoarsely. "We'll freeze!"

His brother sat up and nodded. "Easy, Joe. We'll have to stay calm if we expect to get out of this alive."

Groggy, they stood up and tried to keep their balance in the pitch-black, chilly car. The only sound was the clackety-clack of the wheels. Frank took a small flashlight from his pocket and looked around. Their prison was filled with crates of West Coast lettuce.

Climbing up and over them, Frank presently came to the front wall of the car. It was damp and freezing cold against his hand.

"Joe! I just remembered something," he said hopefully. "We're lucky. This is an old-type car. In the new nitrogen refrigerator units we'd be goners for sure. They have practically no oxygen."

"You're right. This oldie has ice compartments at each end. Bunkers."

"Exactly. The bunkers open into this section near the roof, so the cold air can circulate. What about it?"

"That's our way out. Each bunker has a hatch in the roof, where ice is put in."

By the dim beam of the pocket flashlight, they could see that the open parts of the bunkers were covered by wire.

"If we can only cut through that!" Frank said.

"Here." Joe pulled a knife from a pocket in his dungarees.

Climbing up on the stacked lettuce crates,

Frank began hacking away at the wire screen. With only the small penknife, it took time, but finally he made a hole large enough to crawl through. Perched atop a slippery cake of ice, he reached up for the hatch.

It was tightly locked.

"No luck," he called down in disappointment.

Descending to the floor of the car, he added, "We have only one more chance—the other hatch."

"Let me try this time," Joe suggested.

"Okay. Maybe you'll be luckier than I was." With teeth chattering, Joe sawed away at the wire mesh of the other bunker and worked his way in on top of the ice. Anxiously he glanced up at the hatch. A thin sliver of light showed along one edge.

"Frank!" he shouted exultantly. "This one isn't locked!"

Quickly Joe leaned down over the edge of the bunker and helped Frank climb up into the ice chamber. Together, they pushed at the hatch cover, but it didn't budge.

"Joe! All your might!" Frank urged. "This is our only chance!"

"My hands are so numb I can't even feel the hatch."

"We've got to make it!" Frank gasped.

CHAPTER XIV

Thieves' Camp

BRACING their shoulders and arms beneath the hatch of the refrigerator car, Frank and Joe gave one more mighty heave. This time they forced the cover upward and held it against the rushing wind as they scrambled out.

A blast of air nearly threw them off balance. But it was warm, and felt wonderful against their frigid skin.

"Duck down!" Frank yelled. "Less wind resistance."

The train had topped a long grade, and was speeding now to make up for time lost on the hill. The boys swayed as the freight rounded a long curve.

Frank glanced back through the gathering dust to see if he could spot any familiar landmarks. Checking his watch, he surmised they must have traveled past Spur Gulch.

"Hey!" Joe cried out. "We're slowing down!"

"Good!" returned Frank. "I think our best bet is to hop off and walk back to the Gulch."

Amid the rattle and banging of couplings, the long freight train jarred to a stop.

"Out on the sand!" yelled Joe as he eased down on the smooth surface. A hundred yards down the track Frank followed.

"Now," Frank said, "we have a good hike ahead of us back to Spur Gulch. It's nearly time for our date with Dad."

They had hardly hit their stride along the ties when Frank pulled up short.

"Look over there, Joe. In that patch of woods."

The orange-and-red light of a small campfire flickered through a thick grove of trees.

"Should we take time to see who's there?" Joe asked. "After all, we're late now. That campfire may belong to a gang of hobos."

"On the other hand," Frank reasoned, "Dad might be there."

Frank's argument convinced his brother, and the two boys left the right-of-way.

Careful not to make any noise, the Hardys advanced among the trees. At the far edge of the grove in which the fire was located they paused in the underbrush and peered ahead.

A dozen men were huddled around the fire. Two were eating. The others appeared to have finished their meal and were warming themselves near the blaze.

In the low buzz of conversation someone occasionally would make a wisecrack that provoked a chorus of rough laughter. Presently a deep voice which was raised above the rest gave the Hardys a chance to learn the subject of the men's conversation.

"Well, the boss and his new friend'll be here soon," the man rumbled. "Then the fireworks'll start!"

"We can't wait for them much longer," another voice announced impatiently. "Number 68's due here in a little while."

"These men must be train robbers!" Frank whispered. "They're waiting to wreck Number 68 on the tracks right over there!"

"Then maybe we're not too late," Joe said hopefully. "Dad's probably around here somewhere. Let's get closer to these guys. Maybe we can hear exactly what they're up to."

The boys had crawled forward several feet when Frank gripped his brother's arm, pulling him to a stop. With his other hand cupped around Joe's ear, he whispered:

"It just occurred to me—that fellow mentioned the boss and his new friend. Do you think he could have meant Flint and Turk?"

Edging forward on their knees and elbows, the boys tried to get a better look at the faces of the men in the flickering firelight. One of them, his back to the Hardys, addressed the others.

"Can ya imagine a coupla high school kids holdin' up a deal like this. Well, we don't have to worry about them any longer. Flint said he'd take care of 'em before he got here."

Flint! The boys' deduction had been correct!

"At least," Frank told himself elatedly, "we're on the right track now."

"Me, I'm gettin' tired of waitin'," one of the men grumbled. "The sooner we get at this job, the better. I want to put the grab on those pipes and drills and then blow outta here."

"Sure, Hank," another agreed. "The sooner we get hold of that stuff, the quicker we can set up the diggin'."

"Flint said Number 68's got three cars loaded with the last word in oil rigs," Hank went on. "We'll be rollin' in dough in a few weeks, and by that time it'll all be on the level."

Joe prodded Frank and the older boy knew what he was thinking. The stolen rig was to be set up in Wildcat Swamp after the land had been taken from Mrs. Sanderson!

"No wonder those phony rangers invented that government order for everyone to move out," Frank whispered.

Joe was about to speak when a sudden crackling in the woods startled him.

"Too late to run!" Frank whispered. "Lie flat!"

Face down in the undergrowth, they hugged the dry ground. The sound of heavy footsteps grew nearer. The newcomers passed the boys and approached the campfire. Conversation died abruptly. Frank and Joe looked up momentarily, to see one of the men jump up, draw his pistol, and hurry away.

"Who's there?" he called, advancing to only a few feet from where the boys lay hidden.

Frank and Joe hardly dared to breathe until the challenger's attention was diverted by the two new arrivals who stepped into the firelight.

"What's the matter with you, Sam? Jumpy tonight?" one of them asked in a low, controlled voice. Better dressed than any of the others, he presented an almost distinguished appearance.

The man with him was big and broad-shouldered. Even from where the Hardys lay squinting through the brush, they could see him frowning darkly at the others who now clustered around.

Now Frank and Joe were absolutely sure. The men were indeed the Green Sand prisoners—now without their cowboy disguise and masks!

The boys listened tensely.

"Okay, Flint," replied Sam, ramming his pistol back into its holster. "It's this waiting that gets on my nerves." Then, turning to the others, he added, "Meet your boss, men."

Flint was received enthusiastically. All the gang were eager to get their new job under way and the arrival of the boss meant time for action.

Leading his companion into the center of the

group, Flint said, "Men, I want all of you to meet an old pal of mine—Jesse Turk. He's going to be in on this caper with us."

"That's okay by me," Hank said approvingly. "There's gonna be enough dough for everybody."

"Right!" Flint added. "This job is a lead-pipe cinch. We had a little trouble getting rid of those Hardys. And then that fool fossil hunter."

"What happened to him?" Hank asked.

"He and the fat kid with him are tied up and hidden away in a cave—without food and water."

Involuntarily, the Hardys winced at the reference to their friends' plight. Joe, in sudden anger, started to scramble to his knees, but Frank laid a firm hand on his arm.

"Take it easy, Joe. We can help Cap and Chet more by learning all we can here."

Though Frank had restrained him quickly, Joe's sudden movement had been heard. A tall, hard-bitten member of the gang sprang to his feet.

"Boss, what was that over there? I swear I heard something move."

There was an ominous silence as the others listened, too. The wind had died down and not a leaf stirred. Suddenly the still night rang with a rasping laugh. It came from Turk, and his harsh amusement echoed through the woods. The rest stared at him.

"Flint, I thought you said you had men here!"

he said bitingly. "These guys are nothing but a bunch of scared rabbits!"

There was an immediate and angry muttering among the group of outlaws. Before it could develop into a fight, Flint stepped forward.

"All right, knock it off," he ordered briskly. "You guys have nothing to worry about. Those snooping Hardy kids have frozen to death in a refrigerator car, and their old man is next."

"You got him too?" Hank smirked.

"No, but we heard where he is. This job'll be a cinch now."

His authoritative demeanor having eased the tension, Flint drew Turk and Hank aside in a private conversation, while the others began talking of the robbery plans. Taking advantage of the general chatter, Frank nudged Joe.

"Back out of here," he proposed in a whisper.

Joe nodded and began inching his way backward through the brush. They had to get away—had to get to Spur Gulch, find their father, and warn him.

They had moved about half the distance to the edge of the grove when they heard Flint giving more orders.

"Enough talk, men! Time to get moving. We've got a job to do before we can pull the holdup."

To the boys' horror, the men picked up flashlights and began to tramp through the trees right in their direction.

"They'll spot us this time," Joe groaned. "How are we going to hide from all of them?"

Frank's quick mind hit upon an idea. "Hurry! Up a tree!"

Rapidly, before the beams of the flashlights could reach them, he and Joe picked out two sturdy pine trees with low-hanging branches and shinned up into their thick foliage.

Seconds later the men pushed past beneath them and moved out of earshot.

"That was close," Joe muttered as they climbed down. "Now what?"

"It's better this way," Frank told him. "Now we can trail them."

The boys followed the gang, keeping well concealed. It was hard going without lights in the dark woods, and their pace was slow compared to the men's.

Finally they saw the gang break out of the woods near the summit of the hill on which the boys had jumped off the freight car. Beyond, the roadbed curved and descended in a long horseshoe.

"Let's go over there and watch," Frank said, pointing to a cluster of tall bushes down the tracks from where the men had emerged.

Halfway around the curve of the tracks, the outlaws disappeared into the trees again. A mo-

ment later, when Joe was about to start after
them, they reappeared, their flashlights bobbing
as if they were carrying something.

"What have they got there?" Joe whispered.

"Looks to me like old railroad ties," Frank answered. "But what on earth—?"

His unfinished query was answered immediately as the men heaved the great chunks of wood
onto the tracks and set them afire.

A bright flame licked at the tinder-dry wood,
and in no time it had grown into a crackling blaze.

"Frank, we must warn the engineer!" Joe cried.

The boys started in the direction the freight
would be coming.

But at that moment Flint stepped into their
path and shouted:

"It's burning fine, men. Here comes that rat-
tler. To your jobs!"

Splitting into small groups, his henchmen disappeared into the night. Flint hurried off down
the tracks toward the freight.

"Now's our chance," Joe said. "We may be
caught, but we ought to make a try."

"We'll certainly be caught if we go that way,"
Frank objected. "Let's see if we can push those
burning logs away so the train won't have to
stop."

CHAPTER XV

The Wreck

DASHING uphill as fast as their legs would carry them, the Hardys sped toward the pile of burning ties. Reaching the spot, they found the center a roaring blaze, the heat intense.

Nevertheless, the two boys tugged frantically at the end of one of the heavy ties. At first it would not budge, and the Hardys' faces were scorched before they managed to drag the heavy piece of wood away from the pyre. Its removal caused the others to collapse, sending sparks in every direction.

"It's no use!" Frank panted, beating off the sparks that singed his shirt. "We couldn't clear this away in time."

Their faces and arms smarting, and their eyes bloodshot, they were forced to move back.

"We'll have to try the other plan," Joe urged. "Come on!"

Frank was dubious of its success, but he followed Joe. They hurried forward, jumping from tie to tie.

"I hope none of that gang's watching," Frank said. "If they see us, it's curtains."

Aided by the downgrade, the boys put a quarter mile between them and the fire before they saw the bright beam of the freight train's headlight. As the long train bore down on them with a roar, the Hardys took a determined stance in the middle of the track, waving their arms furiously. A second later the hoarse, warning honk of the Diesel's horn split the night with staccato blasts.

Still the boys held their position. The Diesel's air brakes suddenly were jammed on with a shriek, and the heavy freight ground to a stop. As the Hardys rushed toward the locomotive, the engineer leaned from the window.

"Are you kids crazy?" he bellowed. "You could have been killed! What's the idea?"

"There's danger ahead!" Joe blurted.

"Train robbers!" Frank added.

In a space of a few seconds, the Hardys impressed upon the engineer the necessity for speedy action. Turning, the man seized the induction telephone to the caboose, and frantically tried again and again to contact the men there.

"This is dead!" he cried. "There's no answer!"

Just then, from the other side of the big locomotive, came a rough command:

"Drop that phone and put up your hands!"

The engineer's eyes widened in panic. Letting the instrument fall to the floor, he raised his hands, at the same time trying to nod to the boys to warn them.

There was nothing for Frank and Joe to do but to slip quietly into the brush along the tracks. From this cover, they peered up into the cab.

Two masked men were climbing into the compartment from the other side of the train, holding at gunpoint both the engineer and his fireman. Up the track, other members of the gang were using long hooks to remove the smoldering, red-hot ties.

"If we cut through the woods, we can warn the crew in the caboose ourselves!" Frank urged.

Stumbling blindly through the darkness on the inside of the horseshoe curve, the boys made their way toward the end of the long freight. They tripped over fallen logs, and whiplike branches cut their faces.

"There are the lights of the caboose," Frank gasped. "Keep going!"

Guided by the lights, they broke out of the woods and clambered up a short slope. Joe grabbed for the railing and scrambled up the iron steps. Frank was right behind him. They had barely reached the platform on the tail end of the car when the train gave a lurch.

"We're moving!" Joe yelled.

The next instant a voice, which was strangely familiar, shouted: "Jump!"

The command carried so much authority that the boys obeyed instinctively. Leaping backward, they somersaulted down the cinder-packed embankment. Unhurt, they sprang quickly to their feet.

"The end of the train has broken loose!" Joe shouted.

The caboose and three big flatcars adjoining it had cut free and were rolling downgrade. The rest of the freight had started pulling ahead.

While the front section was slowly picking up speed, the four end cars were gathering momentum every second as they took the downhill curve.

"They'll derail!" Frank shouted. "The whole crew in the caboose will be killed!"

Hardly were the words off his lips when there was the sound of crunching steel, accompanied by flying sparks as the cars leaped the tracks.

With a tremendous roar, the cars toppled over the embankment. Their cargo slid off the toppling flatcars, scattering along the wooded right-of-way.

Several minutes passed before the din made by the falling pipes quieted.

The Hardys started running toward the wrecked caboose, fearful of what they would find.

"We might have been on that!" Joe said.

"Who yelled 'Jump'?" Frank asked.

"Say, I'd forgotten about that," Joe answered.
"Sh-h-h!"

The whispered warning came from behind them. Wheeling about, the boys saw a dim figure half hidden under a bush. A tall, strongly built man beckoned to them.

"Dad!" Frank and Joe exclaimed in unison.

There was no time now to exchange stories. The three raced to the site of the wreck, climbing around scattered pipes and splintered boxes.

"There's the caboose!" Joe called. "The door has been ripped off!"

Quickly all three pushed through the debris to the train crew's headquarters. Pulling themselves up its splintered sides, they peered down into the twisted, torn wreckage.

"There isn't anyone in it!" Mr. Hardy exclaimed. "Thank goodness you boys heard me and jumped."

"But where's the crew?" Joe asked. "The engineer was trying to get someone on the induction phone in his cab."

"They probably jumped out to see what was happening when you boys flagged the train," Mr. Hardy deduced. "They may have been coming up along the embankment when the last four cars started rolling."

"In that case, the crew should be around here somewhere," Frank said.

"Yes, but I doubt very much if they would be a

match for such a large gang as this one. Now the question is, Did those cars break loose, or did someone uncouple them?"

"They were wrecked on purpose," Frank answered, and told his father all that had happened since the shooting down of the radio aerial balloon; how they had overheard that Flint was boss of the gang; how Cap and Chet were prisoners in a cave; and all because the ex-convicts wanted to drill for oil illegally on Mrs. Sanderson's land.

"We'll rescue Chet and Cap as soon as we can," Mr. Hardy decided. "They'll have to hold out awhile. First we must do something about this gang here, and it's going to be tough without help."

"Are you alone, Dad?" Joe asked.

"Sam Radley is out here working with me, but all our tips pointed to Spur Gulch as the trouble spot. He was bringing a posse to meet me there. But now that you've told me about the oil drilling, I can see why Flint picked this place. Those three cars contain the materials they need. There's a rough woods road near here over which they can drag the stuff."

"Dad, how come you're in this spot alone?" asked Frank.

"Jack Wayne flew me in. The only level spot on the mountain was about half a mile from here. I planned to walk to Spur Gulch along the tracks.

"On the way, I came almost face to face with

some of this gang, and couldn't get past them. What I have been doing is taking pictures with our infrared camera of any of these thugs I could get close to. We'll have quite a record of—"

A shot rang out, then another. A moment later two uniformed trainmen came racing in their direction, followed by two of the robbers. Mr. Hardy, whipping out his own revolver, was about to go to the assistance of the trainmen when six more armed outlaws came into view.

"We're outnumbered," the detective said in disgust. "Our only chance to capture that gang now is by a trick."

The Hardys hugged the trees to keep from being seen, but even from his hiding place, the detective kept clicking his camera.

"This is all good evidence," he whispered grimly. "When we get this mob into court, the jury won't take long to convict every one of them."

Frank and Joe had no doubt of their father's ability to outwit the gang eventually, but at this moment the situation looked desperate. Besides, all three of them were in danger of being captured.

"Keep under cover," the detective warned as Joe stepped out. "This is no time to be discovered."

The words were hardly out of his mouth when their hiding place became flooded with light!

CHAPTER XVI

The Rough Ride

Six bright beams of light swept the Hardys' hiding place from the opposite side of the tracks. As they drew closer, they could make out two low-slung open trucks, each with a powerful spotlight, in addition to glaring headlights.

"Great crow!" Joe exclaimed. "Where did they come from?"

"Over the abandoned logging road," his father replied. "More of Flint's smart organization work. Those trucks can carry the pipes and oil-well equipment out of here easily."

"Can't we do something?" Frank asked desperately as the trucks lurched across the rails and halted alongside the wrecked cars.

"I think so," his father said coolly. "I'm going to trick Flint and try to capture him."

The detective turned to his sons. "You boys take note of what's going on here. Wait until the next train passes through. That'll be at nine A.M. The robbers will have left long before that. Stop the train and ride to Red Butte. I'll meet you there at noon."

The detective pulled out a small bottle. "Concentrated food tablets," he said, handing them to Frank. "You may need them."

After saying good-by to his sons, Mr. Hardy crawled through the bushes until he was in heavy cover. Then he stood up cautiously. Returning to the tracks, he walked upgrade a considerable distance from the scene of the robbery.

When the detective was sure he could not be seen by the men loading the boxes and pipes onto the trucks, he crossed the tracks.

Easing back to the scene slowly, he spotted two figures who stood on a rise, silhouetted against the night sky. Mr. Hardy moved within hearing distance.

"Worked like a charm, Turk," one of the men said. "I uncoupled the last four cars and clamped the air brake on the forward section, so the rest of the train could move ahead as soon as Pete got the burned ties off the tracks."

"Flint, you're a brain. We ought to have this load out of here within an hour."

With a grim smile on his lips, Mr. Hardy stepped into the open.

"Flint!" he shouted.

The two train robbers whirled around. The

shutter of the detective's camera clicked twice.
Turk beamed his flashlight as Mr. Hardy ducked.

Flint cursed, whipped a pistol from his shoulder holster, and fired a clip of bullets at the spot where the detective had stood a second before.

"It's Fenton Hardy!" Flint roared. "Turk, you supervise the men. Lend me your light. I'm going to get this dick if it's the last thing I ever do!"

As soon as the detective saw Flint coming after him, he drew back into the wooded area and headed for Jack Wayne's plane. Mr. Hardy deliberately let Flint catch an occasional glimpse of him, leading the gangleader farther away from his men.

Flint's rage increased as the detective tormented him with a dangerous game of cops and robbers. Half an hour later Mr. Hardy emerged from the woods into a clearing, in the center of which stood Jack Wayne's plane. Running toward it, the detective shouted:

"Jack! Flint's right behind me. Cover me while I give him a whiff of the gas gun!"

As a face appeared in the pilot's window, the detective stopped short. Instead of Jack Wayne's familiar features, he saw in the moonlight a thin face with a large sharp nose and eyes like black marbles. An unknown enemy was facing him and Flint was only a few steps behind!

Meanwhile, the detective's sons had continued to watch the well-planned and executed theft of the oil-well drilling equipment. The freight's conductor and brakemen were being kept covered.

In an hour the two trucks were loaded and the cargoes concealed with heavy tarpaulins. Two men climbed into each cab and the others faded into the woods along with their prisoners.

"So long!" one driver called. "See you at Wildcat Swamp after we deliver this stuff to Willie and Nick Snide."

Frank and Joe exchanged glances. No doubt the man meant Willie the Penman. But who was Snide?

The Hardys' nerves tingled. "Frank, are we going to stand here and do nothing?" Joe cried.

"No sir. Come on!" Frank muttered. "We'll ride back to Wildcat Swamp and free Cap and Chet."

"How about meeting Dad?"

"We'll get there—maybe just a bit late."

As the trucks pulled away, the boys ran across the track. Racing down the other side, they found the narrow, overgrown logging road, then began following the second truck's taillights.

Fortunately the loaded vehicles were forced to crawl along the twisting logging road. Jogging alongside, Joe was able to untie a corner of the tarpaulin and boost himself aboard the load of loose steel pipes. He pulled Frank up after him, and the boys retied the canvas over them. As the truck rolled along through the night, Frank whispered:

"From the feel of the grades and turns, we're still on the logging road."

"It's rough going," Joe replied. "I wish they'd picked a smoother route."

With each big lurch and bump, the pipes clanged and slithered into new positions. The boys fought to keep their balance and avoid being pinched between portions of the cargo.

After what seemed hours, the truck groaned to a stop. Another vehicle approached at high speed and roared past, the sound of its whining tires fading in the distance.

"We must have reached the main highway," Frank deduced.

A moment later the truck edged onto a smooth pavement.

"Thank goodness for this," Joe whispered.

The driver shifted into high gear, and the vehicle rumbled along smoothly. Despite the boys' discomfort, the harrowing experiences of the day and night were making them drowsy. After what seemed to be hours, Joe awoke with a start. He reached out and shook his brother's arm.

"Frank! Wake up! We've stopped!"

Joe found a tiny hole in the canvas and peeked through it.

"We're at a diner," he whispered. "The driver

and his helper are going to the door. The other truck is parked ahead of us."

Frank drew his penknife and cut a small peephole. "They're probably stopping for a cup of coffee," he whispered. "When they get inside, let's go in the back way and phone the police.

"Get back! They're coming out!"

The driver and his helper, who was fairly young, approached the truck, accompanied by a third man. As they headed toward the back of the vehicle, the boys eased forward and slid between the pipes and some boxes, just as the tarpaulin was lifted, letting in a slit of light.

"We got it, all right," said a voice the boys recognized as that of the driver. "The whole works."

"What's up there in front?" the man from the diner asked.

The boys held their breath.

"Boxes of drill bits and fittings."

From the men's conversation, it became evident that the newcomer owned the diner. As the cover was tied down again, he said:

"I got a report from Flint already."

"So quick? What'd he say?"

"Buzzed me on his pocket radio. He'll be along soon. Said to tell you that he and Fliegel captured Fenton Hardy and his pilot."

The words came like an electric shock to the

boys. Flint had turned the tables and captured their father!

"Man, that was fast work!" the driver said with a hoarse laugh. "Flint just told us back at the railroad he had a plan for getting Hardy."

"Well, he did it. Must've done a real job on him, too. Flint said the dick needs a doctor, but he ain't getting one! You get started. I'll take a look at the other truck."

Frank and Joe were frantic with worry. Their father was injured and needed help, and here they were, powerless to aid him.

As the truck started along the highway again, Joe said, "Frank, we'd better get off the first chance we have. We'll find a ranch house and call the police. We've got to find Dad!"

"You're right."

The boys watched through the holes in the canvas. But they passed no ranch houses and the truck sped through the night at high speed. The boys heard the driver's helper say to his companion:

"You know, I don't trust that flat-nosed Snide. I think he'd double-cross the lot of us in a minute, if he had the chance."

Joe's elbow dug into Frank's side. Flat-nosed! One of the phony rangers had a flat nose!

"But you gotta remember, Charlie," the driver was saying, "Snide's a good oilman. He'll be useful to have around."

There was a snort from his companion.

"I don't care—I'd rather do without him. He's too ready to go to extremes. He woulda killed one of those kids without battin' an eye, and I just can't go that far."

"Aw, can it! Anybody gets in our way deserves what he gets."

There was a growl of disagreement from the younger man, but apparently he could not see much sense in continuing the argument. The men lapsed into silence.

"That young helper doesn't sound like such a bad sort," Frank whispered to Joe. "I wonder how he got mixed up with a gang like this."

They felt the truck slow down and turn off the smooth highway onto a bad road. The wheels alternately crunched over loose stone and slid through soft sand.

It was perilous going. The Hardys were forced to move from behind the crates and crouch on top of the load. As the truck hit a bad bump, the younger man shouted:

"Hey, watch it! This ain't no superhighway!"

"Calm down," the driver said irritably. "It's only ten miles to the swamp, Charlie."

"Just the same," Charlie said, "there ain't no reason to set a record. We passed the other truck an hour ago."

The truck lurched over, its right wheels slipping sideways. "Watch that ditch!"

"Aw, shut up! You been a pain in the neck ever since we started this job."

"I don't like what's goin' on. If—"

His words were cut off as the big vehicle skidded. The load shifted sharply, sending an avalanche of pipe toward Frank and Joe!

CHAPTER XVII

A Friendly Outlaw

"Look out, Frank!" The warning shout slipped from Joe involuntarily.

Reaching high, the boys grabbed the cross braces, and pulled themselves up just as the heavy sections of pipe crashed across the floor of the truck.

The big vehicle skidded to the side of the road, shuddering as it hit the soft shoulder, and stalled.

"Now you've done it," they heard the helper berate the driver. "If we get stuck here, the boss'll—"

"Shut up!" the angry driver commanded. "Didn't you hear that yell? Somebody's in the back of this truck!"

"Aw, you're loco."

"Listen, bud, I heard somethin', and I'm checkin' up."

With a mad scramble Frank and Joe slid from

under the tarpaulin and landed in the road. Quietly they ducked underneath the truck's chassis, just as the husky driver swaggered down from the cab.

He walked along the side of the truck to the rear, the boys watching his feet every step of the way. Leaning over the tailboard, he fumbled with the canvas tarpaulin. Joe looked at the man's legs, so near his own hidden shoulder.

"Too good to miss!" he thought.

Reaching out his arms, he grabbed the back of the driver's legs and yanked them forward. There was a startled *umph* as the fellow went crashing to the road. His gun went one way and his flashlight another. Before he could yell to his helper, the two boys were upon him. Joe sent his fist swinging hard to the man's jaw, and he collapsed without a sound.

Quickly the boys dragged his inert form under the truck. They were not a second too soon.

"Well, did you find anythin'?" Charlie called as he climbed out of the cab.

Receiving no answer, he stalked to the rear of the vehicle to investigate. Frank set himself to duplicate his brother's action. His shoulder hit the man just below the knees, and before Charlie knew what was happening to him, Joe dealt him a knockout blow.

"What are we going to do with them?" Joe asked.

"I don't know yet, but we'll have to do something fast. Look!"

Down the road, still a good distance away, two bouncing pinpoints of light became visible. The other truck was catching up with them!

"Come on. We'll drag these fellows into the tall grass there." Frank indicated the high growth on the other side of the road, and quickly they tugged the two unconscious men out of sight.

"We'd better run," Joe advised.

Frank had another plan. "We don't want them to stop. Let's put on their caps and pull 'em down. They'll hide our faces a little, and maybe we can get by."

"All right. You get in the cab. I'll pretend I'm tying this canvas, and you wave them on from the window," Joe suggested.

By this time the beams of the other truck's headlights were almost upon them. Frank climbed as casually as he could into the cab and sat there with his left hand giving the passing signal. Joe fussed with the canvas on the side of the truck opposite to where the other vehicle would pass.

Those few seconds seemed an eternity to the boys as the second truck rolled up to them, but fortunately it did not slow down. There was a shouted ridicule about "lazy coyotes," but the driver kept his foot pressed down on the accelerator.

The driver went crashing to the road

The scheme had worked!

"We'd better get back to those two we hid and tie them before they wake up," Frank said, leaping from the cab.

Using the rope with which the canvas had been tied, they first secured the driver's wrists and ankles. Just as he was coming to, they managed to gag him firmly.

"We'd better drag him back where there's no possible chance of his rolling into the road and having one of the gang find him," Frank proposed.

The driver was dragged off and wedged into a cluster of trees.

"How about Charlie?" Joe asked. "I'll get more rope."

"Wait!" Frank said. "I've been thinking about Charlie. He sounded as if he's fed up with the gang. Do you suppose we could persuade him—?"

The young man was just beginning to show signs of regaining consciousness when the boys returned to him. Frank removed Charlie's pistol a split second before he sat up and shook his head.

"What happened?" he groaned.

When his head had cleared, the boys revealed their identity.

"But I thought you were—"

"Frozen to death in that refrigerator car?" Joe finished grimly. "No, your boss just wasn't smart enough."

"I'm glad of that!" Charlie growled. "I told those hombres they were goin' too far."

"Listen, Charlie," Frank began earnestly, "you don't seem to be a bad sort. Why don't you quit this gang right now?"

"You could go straight, and give us a hand in the bargain," Joe urged.

"How?" Charlie asked suspiciously.

"If you help us turn the tables on those thieves, we'll do everything we can to clear you with the police."

"But if you stick with them," Frank said, "the way things are going, they're bound to wind up in prison for life."

Charlie was silent, looking first at the Hardys and then off into the distance, as he thought the proposition over.

"You're right," he said at last. "Now's my chance. Maybe you won't believe me, but I just hooked up with Flint. Lure of easy money. I ain't done anythin' yet to get me a sentence." He paused a few seconds. "I got two kid brothers your age. If I get caught now—well, I guess I'll have to trust you about helpin' me out. But first, what can I do?"

Elated over this unexpected source of assistance, the boys helped Charlie to his feet and discussed the situation.

"Somebody's got to find out about our dad," Frank said. "Flint radioed that fellow back at the diner that Dad needed a doctor. He must be hurt! Where's Flint?"

"He's goin' to the diner," Charlie answered. "We're all supposed to meet there later."

"How about you going back there and finding out about my father?" Frank asked. "Then you can notify the police."

"And the driver? Can you take care of him?" Joe asked.

"I'll send somebody out to bring him in," Charlie promised. "Don't worry. You can count on me. I don't want to end up in the chair!"

It was decided that the boys would drive on to the swamp, while Charlie would walk to the main highway and hitch a ride back to the diner. As proof of the boys' confidence in him, Frank gave the man his gun.

Charlie set off down the rough trail and the boys climbed into the cab of the truck.

"How close do you think we ought to get to that gang?" Joe asked.

"Not too close. We'll sneak up on foot and find out where they're taking this equipment."

"Then we'll head for the cave to help Cap and Chet," Joe added as the truck bumped and jounced along.

After that, the boys rode in silence until they saw lights ahead. Frank slowed the truck to a crawl.

"They're unloading the stuff," he said. "I

would guess they are at the top of the slope above Wildcat Swamp, just opposite where we were digging."

Several men were busy carrying lengths of pipe and heavy boxes which they were piling behind some bushes. Fortunately no one turned around when Frank braked to a complete stop.

"Now's our chance to get away!" Joe urged. They quickly climbed out and hurried into the shadows.

By this time streaks of gray were showing in the eastern sky. With the breaking dawn to help them, the boys picked their way toward the swamp. Knowing that the thieves would be camping somewhere near it, they gave the area a wide berth as they made their way toward the sloping bank where they had been digging.

They were skirting the swamp when Joe suddenly stopped to listen. In the distance there was a low hum and rumble.

"The trucks, Frank! They must have finished unloading. They're leaving."

"I hope Charlie gets to the diner before they do. That gang's surely discovered by this time that he and the driver are missing. They're probably searching for them right now."

The boys pushed on around the swamp, finally completing a tortuous half circle that brought them to the bottom of the sandy slope in which the camel fossil was buried.

"Say," said Joe as he reached the entrance to the cave, "what have they done to this place? It's choked with sand and rocks!"

"The gang must have done it to hide the entrance from strangers," Frank replied. "I wonder if the other entrance—"

They rushed around to the other end of the slope. The entrance there had been blocked in exactly the same way.

"This is worse," Joe announced. "I think the other entrance will be easier to negotiate."

They returned to it, scrambling over the pile of sand and gravel to reach the cave opening. Before entering, Frank played the strong beam of his flashlight as far into the cave as it would carry.

"Cap! Chet!" Joe called.

There was no answer.

"Come on, Frank!"

After a breath-taking slide, they landed in the mouth of the deep cavern, and flashed their lights around. There was no sign of Cap and Chet.

Dismayed and filled with apprehension, Frank began a search of the inner area. "There may be a deeper section to this cave than we thought."

Seconds later Joe heard his cry of joy. "They're here!"

Lying in a crevice beneath the far wall, bound and gagged, were their friends. In no time, the Hardys had Cap and Chet out in the central portion of the cave.

"I'll get the gags off," Joe said excitedly. "You untie their hands."

With his pocketknife he sliced the tight kerchiefs with which the captives had been gagged. Even when the gags were removed, Cap and Chet could barely whisper. They were very weak, saying they had had no food since being captured.

After all their bonds were removed, the two found that because of their long inactivity, they could not stand up. Frank and Joe massaged their numbed arms and legs to restore circulation, and in a little while the released prisoners were able to hobble painfully.

"Eat some of these food tablets," Frank said. "They'll help until we can get some solid food."

A few minutes later Cap and Chet were able to give a halting, whispered account of their capture by the phony rangers.

The Hardys burned with anger when they were told that the outlaws had come back a second time to gag their captives and bind them even more securely.

"It was then," Cap continued with parched lips, "that they tried to seal off the entrances to the cave. They said nobody, not even the Hardys, would see us alive again."

"I'd like to get my hand on that Willie just once more," Chet muttered.

"Easy does it," Joe advised. "Come on now. We have to get out of here."

It took a long time for Frank and Joe to get their friends out of the sand-choked passageway, but eventually all four stood on the ledge at the slope. Cap and Chet, accustomed for so long to the darkness of the cave, were almost blinded by the early-morning light.

"Listen, Frank," said Joe, "they're in no condition to walk. I'll get their horses, while you stay here with them."

Cap laid a hand on Frank's arm.

"No use!" he said in a discouraged, tired voice. "The men took our horses. We're stranded!"

CHAPTER XVIII

Trapped!

FRANK shot a startled glance at Joe. The Hardys knew the seriousness of the situation and Cap sensed it too.

"You boys go ahead to Red Butte," he told them. "Chet and I will take it easy and get there when we can."

"But the horses," Chet spoke up. "You can't go far in this country without horses."

"Our pack mule," Joe cried. "He was well hidden. If the thieves didn't take him, Frank and I will ride to Red Butte and send horses back."

"Our nearest point to contact the law," Cap suggested, "is Sheriff Paul."

"We never did find out what happened at his home," Frank reminded his brother. "Suppose we see if he's returned. On their way back to Red Butte, Cap and Chet can stop at the Sanderson ranch to see if everything is all right there."

Leaving Cap and Chet, the Hardys made for

the campsite to look for the pack animal. It was grazing in a little natural corral. The boys threw a blanket across the mule's back and mounted.

For a moment the mule stood still; then, at a signal from Frank's heel, it plodded up the slope. Reaching the trail, the animal ignored a signal to turn right and doggedly trudged toward Wildcat Swamp. No amount of coaxing could change its mind.

"Now what are we going to do?" Joe asked impatiently.

"It's just possible," Frank reflected, "that our mule has been used by someone else and is taking the route he's become accustomed to. He may lead us to a new clue."

The boys rode along without attempting to guide the animal. It headed straight for the defile, went through it, and stopped just above the spot where Cap and the boys had been digging.

"Well, what do you make of this?" Joe asked, perplexed.

Frank jumped off and started down the slope, waving to Joe to follow.

"Somebody else has been digging here—they even put up a sign!" he cried.

" 'Danger,' " he read aloud. " 'Explosives buried. Keep out.' "

"I wonder if that's a trick to scare people away from here," Joe pondered.

"We'd better not stop to find out," Frank re-

plied. "But I think we should warn Chet and Cap
in case it's true."

This time the mule willingly carried the boys in
the opposite direction. Reaching camp, he turned
in.

"Somebody sure has been using this mule recently," Frank said. "I wonder if it was to carry
dynamite."

"Sure looks like it—if the sign means anything," Joe answered.

At that moment Cap and Chet wearily arrived
at the camp.

"What's up now? I see you found the mule, but
why did you come back?" Chet asked.

Quickly the Hardys explained and urged their
friends to stay away from the pit.

When Cap agreed, Frank and Joe started off
again. Reaching the trail, their mule once more
turned left.

"Oh, no, not again," Joe cried, trying his best to
guide the animal to the right.

"Now what?" Frank pondered. "It's a long walk
to Sheriff Paul's."

Joe broke a leafy twig from a sapling and re-
mounted. "Frank, you walk ahead the way we
want to go. I'll see what I can do from here."

His brother took the lead rope and started. The
mule walked four steps, then stopped. Joe tickled
its ear with the twig. As the mule's attention was
distracted, Frank coaxed it a few feet farther.

The boys continued this maneuver until the animal seemed to lose interest in going back. There was no more trouble and Frank climbed up behind his brother.

Meanwhile, Cap and Chet were at a loss. Without horses they certainly would not be able to go far.

Sitting before their tent, Cap's far-roving eye spotted a movement on the hillside.

"What are you looking at?" Chet asked.

"I'm not sure, but I'm beginning to work up a hunch," Cap said. "Come with me."

As they scrambled down the incline, Cap let out a cry. "I was right! Our horses!"

The two mounts were tethered in a grove of pine trees.

"So this is where those phony rangers hid them!" Chet exclaimed.

"Now we can do a little traveling of our own!" Cap cheered. "Let's get started for the Sanderson ranch."

Stiffly they swung into the saddles, and a minute later were loping along the trail.

While all this was happening, Frank and Joe were still swaying from side to side on the back of the mule. Without a horse to follow, the mule ambled along at a pace of his own choosing.

After three hours of stumbling over sand-covered rocks and sliding along bare shale, the mule brought the boys in sight of the sheriff's ranch.

"I hope somebody's here," Joe said, "to give me a tall glass of water."

Dismounting, the boys tied the mule behind the barn and went to the door of the ranch house.

"Hello!" they called. No answer.

"Looks exactly as it was before," Frank said, pushing the door open.

Seeing their note lying on the table, the boys went through to the kitchen. The unwashed dishes still rested in the sink and the basket of clothes remained untouched.

"It's obvious that Mrs. Paul hasn't been back here," Joe said. "Shall we start for Red Butte?"

"Yes, but through open country. I don't want to be trapped again."

As the two boys crossed the living room, Joe noticed something strange. "Say, the radiotelephone's gone," he said.

"That means somebody *has* been here since we left," Frank stated.

Before the Hardys could ponder the riddle further, a distant clatter of hoofs caused them to glance out the window. Three riders in green uniforms were galloping up to the house.

"The fake rangers!" Frank warned. "We'd better get out of here."

The boys hurried through the kitchen, closing the back door quietly behind them, then crossed the yard rapidly and hid inside the stone-and-rail corral attached to the barn.

No sooner had they concealed themselves than the men galloped up and dismounted. Through a crack in the corral fence, the boys could see that one of the men was short, wiry, beady-eyed Willie the Penman! The flat-nosed, fierce-looking man with the craggy brows obviously was Snide.

Willie gave a laugh of satisfaction. "This is a snap with the sheriff out of the way, Snide," he said. "He sure bit on that 'missing rangers' gag."

"Willie," Snide said, "I have to hand it to you. The sheriff walked right into that one. Nobody'd ever look for him in the tower."

Nudging his brother, Joe whispered, "I wonder where this tower is they're talking about."

Willie's whining voice continued. "We can't stick around here long. I'll get those seals I'll need to make the papers look legal. Somebody might— in fact, somebody *is* coming. It's that Sanderson kid. Quick! Take off those uniforms. Pretend you're waiting for the sheriff. I'll hide in the barn."

Frank and Joe watched Willie's companions strip off the rangers' uniforms, revealing cowboy outfits underneath. Willie carried the discarded clothes through the open barn door.

Harry rode up to the men, who greeted him in a friendly manner.

"I'm looking for the sheriff," the boy said. "I need his help."

"We're waiting for Paul ourselves," Snide answered. "What's your trouble?"

Frank and Joe clenched their fists, hoping the boy would say no more. But Harry continued earnestly:

"Well, a couple of days ago two boys promised me they'd help Mom find a way to keep her land. They had a campsite near Devil's Swamp and have disappeared. I want Sheriff Paul to help me find them."

"No use," Snide said. "Those boys named Frank and Joe told me they were going back to their home in a place called Bayport. You might as well go home yourself. Just wasting your time here."

Harry looked surprised when he heard the Hardys mentioned, but still seemed undecided. "I've got to see the sheriff," he insisted.

"I'll give him your message, kid."

"Well, okay." The boy wheeled his horse and rode slowly past the corral on his way out.

"Now's my chance," Joe whispered to Frank.

Crouching low and running as quietly as possible he came to the far corner just as Harry did and peered through the bars.

"Pretend you don't see me, Harry," he said in a loud whisper. The boy stiffened. "This is Joe Hardy. Get off your horse and act as if you're tightening the cinch."

Without looking toward Joe's hiding place, the boy dismounted and began adjusting his saddle.

"You've got to get to Red Butte for help," Joe continued. "These men are in with the gang that's after your land! They're holding Sheriff Paul in a tower. Hurry!"

Harry played his part well. He nodded slightly, mounted his horse, and trotted away. Leaving the ranch, he spurred the animal into a gallop. Harry rode at breakneck speed for a mile, then slowed down to rest his horse.

About to resume his fast pace, Harry saw two riders approaching. They guided their horses on either side of him and one man grabbed his reins.

"Whoa, there, kid!" the larger of the two husky riders said. "Where are you going in such a rush?"

"To town," Harry blurted out. "There's a gang of crooks trying to steal Mom's land and they're holding Sheriff Paul a prisoner!"

"How'd you find all this out?" the other man asked.

"Joe Hardy told me. He and his brother Frank are hiding at the ranch right now. You've got to help us!"

"Oh, we'll give you a hand, all right." He turned to his big companion. "Give him both hands!"

The man seized Harry's wrists and tied them behind his back. He lashed the boy around the waist to the pommel of his saddle and hobbled his horse with a length of rope. The animal would be able to move only a few inches with each stop.

Harry's eyes were wide with fright. "What's the idea? You must be—"

"That's right, kid," the big man said. "You talk too much to the wrong people."

Leaving Harry helpless, the men then whipped their horses and galloped on toward the Paul ranch.

Back in the corral, Frank and Joe were still crouching behind the fence. Willie the Penman had gone into the ranch house, but the others remained outside.

There was the clatter of hoofbeats.

"Two men!" Joe whispered, peering between the bars at a pair of riders cantering toward the house. "They can't be reinforcements sent by Harry. It's too soon for that."

When Willie and his henchmen recognized the newcomers, they stepped out to meet them. The men spoke in low tones that did not carry to the corral fence.

"This doesn't look good!" Joe warned. "Look! They're fanning out all over the place as if to cut off our escape."

"Snide is coming this way!" Frank exclaimed, crouching lower.

Stalking cautiously around the corner of the fence where Joe had talked to Harry, Snide turned along its near side. As he reached the end, the boys quietly retreated toward the barn. A few yards more and they could make a run for it.

Suddenly there was a shout from behind them.

"There they are!"

Whirling, the boys found two big cowboys between them and the barn.

Snide ran toward them from the other side.

Frank and Joe were trapped!

CHAPTER XIX

To the Rescue

SNIDE, seeing the Hardys, twisted his mouth to one side and called:

"Come on, Willie!"

The wiry little figure of Willie the Penman rounded the corner, followed by a hulking cowboy.

Frank and Joe delivered a couple of stiff punches, but the odds were against them. The battle was over almost before it began.

Wiping the sweat from his face, Willie stood before Frank and Joe, held firmly in viselike grips by his companions.

"So you got out of the cooler, eh?" he whined. "Well, wise guys, you won't outsmart us again!"

Turning to the other men, he ordered, "Tie 'em up—tight!"

Two men went to the barn and returned with lengths of bailing wire. Twisting it roughly around the boys' wrists and ankles, they made certain that Frank and Joe could not move.

Willie said to Snide, "I'm ready to take off. Just be sure these kids don't pull any fast ones."

"Don't worry," Snide replied. "They're going to stay put."

"Okay. I'm late now. Mrs. Sanderson will be heartbroken if I don't keep our little date."

"Sure you got all the papers for her to sign, Willie?" Snide asked. "Now that we're getting this close, we don't want no slip-up with the law."

"I'm no amateur," Willie said, annoyance in his voice. "She'll sign everything legal and proper. If she don't, I'll tell her about Harry!"

The boys looked at each other in mystified silence. What had Willie meant? Was Harry Sanderson in trouble? If so, that would mean he had not delivered their message for help.

Willie called for one of the horses and rode off in the direction of the Sanderson ranch.

The rest watched until he was out of sight, whereupon Snide turned to the Hardys.

He prodded Joe with a foot. "How'd you jerks get here, anyway?" he rasped.

Receiving no answer, he continued, "Oh, more heroic guys, eh, like your friends in the cave?"

He was interrupted by a sudden shout. "Hey, here's how the bozos got here!"

One of the cowboys appeared from behind the barn, leading the mule. "Ain't this the critter we snatched?" Snide asked. "We'll use him to carry more dynamite," he added. "Let's move."

"Where to?"

"We'll hit the swamp and check up on the oil-rig stuff before we start drilling."

Frank was thrown over the front of Snide's horse, and Joe against the pommel of a cowboy's mount. Doubled up in this uncomfortable manner, they were carried toward Wildcat Swamp.

By the time they came in view of the ridge overlooking the swamp, the boys were aching in every muscle.

"Keep these kids tied up," Snide ordered, "and haul 'em down with us."

The party descended from the narrow ledge toward the pit in which the fossils lay. There, still firmly in place, was the ominous sign: DANGER. EXPLOSIVES BURIED.

"One move out of you guys, and you're dead pigeons," Snide warned. "This place is loaded."

Frank and Joe were dragged from the horses. They were made to sit down on the ground, with their backs against rock shafts. Then they were securely tied to the shafts.

In plain sight, across the swamp, sloped the heavily wooded mountain. Barely jutting above it, like a tiny cheesebox, was the old fire tower.

Frank and Joe shared the same flash of understanding. This must be the tower Willie had mentioned back at the sheriff's ranch.

Twisting slightly, Joe tried to catch Frank's eye. But the movement arrested Snide's attention.

"Listen!" he growled. "I warned you two about moving around. Cut it out! We want you alive when your father gets here. Then we'll take all three of you to the tower and—"

Boom!

The blast thundered between the hills that surrounded Wildcat Swamp, echoing over the valley. Snide's flat nose purpled in growing anger.

"What idiot set off that dynamite ahead of time?" he roared. "I'll break his fool neck."

"Not *that* fool's neck," one of the cowboys said sardonically. "He probably blew himself to bits."

"Yeah? Well, we're lucky that mountain's still there! What you cowpokes don't know about explosives would fill a book!"

"Don't get upset, Snide," the cowboy said reassuringly. "There's plenty more dynamite left."

"I'll check on that myself," Snide said importantly. "And maybe we won't put off the business of the tower any more, either. We can take care of the Hardys another way."

The outlaws mounted their horses, and, riding down the slope toward the edge of the swamp, soon were out of sight.

Frank and Joe looked at each other. "If they stay away long enough, Cap and Chet may come here and rescue us," Joe said.

"I sure hope so!" Frank said.

"Do you believe that stuff about explosives being buried here?" Joe queried.

"They sure didn't seem to walk around very carefully," Frank observed. "And even if there is dynamite buried here, I don't believe it can be set off just by stepping on it. They were hoping to scare us into sitting still."

"I guess you're right—and that means we can try to get loose!"

Encouraged by this idea, they struggled hard with their bonds.

"Try rubbing the wire up and down on the rock," Joe suggested. "Maybe it'll snap."

But this was a hopeless effort. Every movement they made only rubbed skin off their wrists. Time dragged on and nobody came.

Frank had lapsed into thoughtful silence. He began going over the entire mystery, step by step. When his mind conjured up the picture of the three phony rangers, dressed in their ill-fitting uniforms, he suddenly exclaimed:

"Joe, we have to get over to that tower, pronto!"

"Why?"

"I have a hunch," Frank said excitedly. "From what Snide said, I figure three real rangers are imprisoned there—and Sheriff Paul, too!"

"I get it," Joe said. "The men whose uniforms they stole."

"Right," Frank continued, "and after Willie

got all the papers signed, the rangers were going to be released. But not now. I think we've forced their hand."

"How?"

"We came along and found out what's going on," Frank reasoned. "Now those thieves will have to do away with every one of us."

Cap and Chet, meanwhile, still sore and stiff after their captivity in the cave, were riding toward the Sanderson ranch house. Approaching it, Chet pointed to a horse tethered in front.

"That's not Harry's," he said, reining in.

"Then we'd better find out who's here before we barge in," Cap decided.

"If we tie our horses among these trees," Chet suggested, "we can slip up to the house from the other side of the barn and look in."

It took several minutes for them to circle around and approach the place from its blind side. Peering from the shadow of the adjacent barn, neither Cap nor Chet could see anyone. Stealthily they tiptoed across the yard and crept to an open window.

Cap cautiously raised his head until his eyes were on a level with the sill. He peered into the Sanderson living room. Almost immediately he ducked, turned, and waved to Chet to take a look.

Chet's hurried glance revealed Willie the Penman, seated at a table with Mrs. Sanderson. The forger was handing her a pen.

"You may as well sign this document," Willie was saying, "and get it over with."

"Oh, I wish my husband were still alive!" Mrs. Sanderson sobbed. "He'd know what to do."

"Harry says it's best," came Willie's high-pitched tones. "And he talked it over with those Hardy kids."

Cap's hand tightened on Chet's shoulder. The science teacher pointed to the ranch-house door, standing ajar. Silently they crept to the entrance.

"Oh, all right, give me the pen. I'll sign," they heard the bewildered woman say resignedly.

"Now!" Cap commanded, and charged into the house with Chet behind him.

Like twin thunderbolts, they landed on Willie's back. Surprised, the wily criminal tried desperately to pull his gun. But Chet knocked it across the room. Ten seconds later Willie was stretched out helpless on the floor.

"Don't be frightened!" Cap told Harry's terrified mother. "We're friends of the Hardy boys," and he introduced himself and Chet. "This forger," he went on, "has been trying to bilk you out of your land."

After Cap had explained the situation to Mrs. Sanderson, the woman burst into tears of relief.

"Have you seen Harry?" she asked.

Before Cap or Chet could answer, Willie suddenly spoke up. "I know where he is! In trouble! And so are Frank and Joe Hardy."

"Where are they?" Cap demanded.

"Will you let me go if I tell you? Give me a half hour's start, and I promise I won't go back to the gang. And I'll tell you how to save the three kids."

Cap and Chet looked at each other, then at Mrs. Sanderson.

"Can we believe him?" she asked.

"I wouldn't trust this man any farther than I can throw him!" Chet said. "He'd go right to the gang and warn them, and there's no telling what they'd do to our friends."

"He's right," Cap said to Mrs. Sanderson.

Just then there was the sound of hoofbeats outside. Hurrying to the window, the woman exclaimed, "It's Mrs. Paul and two deputies!"

The sheriff's wife said she was searching for her husband. "I'm afraid he's lying hurt somewhere, so I asked Bill and Ted to help me find him."

"Why don't you stay with me?" Mrs. Sanderson suggested. "Bill and Ted can take this thief to Red Butte and lock him up."

Cap, who did not put much stock in Willie's dire assertion, nevertheless asked the deputies to find out if the Hardys had reached Red Butte. He and Chet would go back to the fossil pit in case Frank and Joe should return.

"And please look for Harry," Mrs. Sanderson begged the deputies.

The lawmen nodded and left with their glowering prisoner. Chet asked Mrs. Sanderson if they might borrow some tools, and after getting them, he and Cap started for the fossil area.

Meanwhile, Frank and Joe, sitting against the rocks to which they were bound, heard furtive footsteps in the defile above them.

"Somebody's coming!" Joe warned.

Listening intently, they heard the clatter of a dislodged stone. Then, as a head came cautiously into view around the ledge, Frank and Joe shouted in relief.

"Harry Sanderson! Hurry up and untie us!"

While untwisting the Hardys' wire bonds, Harry was told what had happened to them. Then he in turn related the story of his own capture.

"How'd you get loose?" Frank asked.

"Rolled off my horse and cut the ropes on a sharp rock. I figured it would be too late to get help for you boys. So I rode back to the Paul ranch. When I saw all the hoofprints headed this way, I was sure you were prisoners, so I came along."

After the Hardys had told Harry the news about Willie, Joe pointed to the old fire tower.

"Our problem," he said, "is to get to that place without horses. We think the sheriff and three rangers are being held up there."

"It's not as great a problem as you think," Harry said. "I know a safe way through the swamp. Follow me." He hid his horse in a thicket and set out on foot.

Harry's route to the tower was surprisingly short. He seemed to have an uncanny knowledge of the bog, leading the Hardys along high spots and across a series of hummocks. Soon the three stood at the foot of the mountain and looked up.

It seemed like an impossible climb, but the boys started up the steep slope on hands and knees. Sharp rocks cut their boots, and saplings which they grabbed for support pulled out of the thin soil. Finally they clambered to the flat stretch of ground on which the fire tower was built.

The gray, rickety wooden structure, standing in the center of a clearing bounded by scrubby trees, seemed to be deserted.

The boys looked around for possible guards, but none were in sight. Cautiously the three advanced and went to the door in the base of the tower. It had been forced open and hung by one hinge.

Frank and Joe stepped gingerly inside. Harry followed.

"Stand guard," Frank told the boy. "Yell if anyone shows up, then run to a safe place."

Harry took up a position behind the broken door as Frank and Joe started to climb the creaking wooden stairway.

"I hope these steps hold us, Joe!"

The stairs clung to the wall, ascending in steep, right-angled turns. At each step the Hardys took, the tower trembled.

Finally they reached the floor of the observation tower. No one was there.

"Guess we were wrong," said Joe.

"Maybe not."

Gazing at the ceiling, Frank noticed that the boards did not match exactly.

"Joe! I believe there's a trap door up there! Give me a boost."

As Frank climbed to Joe's shoulders, there was a sudden pounding above him. Then muffled cries of "Help! Help!"

Frank put his shoulder against the trap door and heaved. It yielded and he pulled himself up through the opening.

A strange sight greeted him. On the floor lay four unshaven, disheveled men, securely bound, but without gags. Three of them wore ill-fitting shirts and trousers. The fourth, a blond, ruddy man, was dressed in blue jeans, a plaid shirt, and a vest with a sheriff's silver star on it.

As Frank pulled Joe up through the opening, the man with the star greeted them weakly. "I'm Sheriff Paul. These men are rangers."

"We're Frank and Joe Hardy. You have to get out of here—fast!" Joe said quickly. "The tower may be blown up any minute!"

With lightning speed, they unbound the prisoners and helped them down to the observation tower. The released men, hardly able to stand, crawled down the stairway.

As they made the perilous descent, Frank and Joe asked, "Who brought you here, Sheriff?"

"All I know is that I received a phone call about some missing rangers. When I went to investigate, three men jumped me."

"Our dad's been captured, too," Frank said as they neared the base of the tower. "He was after a gang of train robbers when they got him."

"Is Fenton Hardy your dad?"

When the boys nodded, the sheriff said warmly, "Mr. Hardy has a great reputation among us lawmen. I sure hope no harm has come to him."

The minutes required to reach the bottom of the tower seemed like hours, but finally Joe hit the last step. Harry's eyes popped when he saw the sheriff and the rangers. When the boy reported that nobody had come in view, Frank urged, "Quick! Run for it. This place may be dynamited any minute!"

No sooner had they dashed through the doorway to the edge of the clearing than they heard an ominous rumble.

"Down!" Frank shouted. "Cover up!"

As they pitched themselves headlong, the earth behind them split open with a shattering roar. The tower bulged at the bottom and started to collapse.

CHAPTER XX

The Roundup

"SAFE!"

Sheriff Paul's whisper broke the silence after the tremendous blast and crash of the tower.

As they all looked back in awe at the mass of debris, one of the rangers said, "If we'd even been in the clearing, we might have been killed."

"The danger isn't over yet," Sheriff Paul reminded them. "That gang will be coming up to check on their job. Let's put some distance between them and us!"

Hurriedly the group moved cautiously down the steep slope, finally stopping to rest in a quiet glade near the base of the mountain.

"With Chet and Cap out of the cave, the next step is to find Dad," Frank proposed.

Then the brothers told about their escape from the refrigerator car, the train wreck, and the capture of one of the truck drivers. When they related how they had persuaded Charlie, the driver's helper, to help them, the sheriff showed keen interest.

"You say his name is Charlie? Say, that might be Charlie Brace, one of the local boys here."

When the Hardys described their new ally, the sheriff nodded. "That's Charlie, all right. A nice young fellow, but he's been getting mixed up with a bad crowd lately."

"Well, now he's going straight," Joe said. "At least we hope he is."

After discussing what their next move should be, it was decided that they would go to the site where the oil-drilling equipment was cached.

"No doubt we'll find some of the gang there," the sheriff observed, "and maybe we can surprise them and nab a few at a time."

They had barely started in the direction of the gang's stockpile when they heard the distant rumble of a motor.

"Sounds like a heavy truck," Joe said.

"Must be on that old logging trail over the next rise," the sheriff said. "Hurry. We'll see who it is."

Careful to conceal themselves in the natural cover, they reached the old trail in time to see a truck stop a short distance away. The driver hopped out.

"Charlie!" the Hardys gasped, and Sheriff Paul nodded. Had he kept his promise? the boys wondered as they watched his actions.

The young fellow seemed to be waving at someone he could see through the trees. Four men emerged from the woods to join Charlie in the road.

Turk, Snide, and two others!

For a couple of minutes the five men stood talking in the center of the road.

Suddenly the back gate of the truck fell with a clatter—and out poured a swarm of men!

Frank's eye caught the foremost of the new arrivals. "Dad!" he shouted.

"Jack Wayne and Sam Radley!" Joe yelled in astonishment.

At the same time the detective's posse surrounded Turk, Snide, and the other two outlaws, disarming them and snapping handcuffs on each of them.

Charlie had kept his promise!

Overjoyed, the onlookers emerged from their hiding place. For a moment, all was confusion as Fenton Hardy greeted his sons and their friends.

"But, Dad, we thought you were hurt!" Frank exclaimed.

"No. Jack and I had a rough time, but we won the fight at the plane. Then I made Flint broadcast the story about our capture, to throw the rest of the gang off. Flint's in jail, and so is Snake Fliegel."

"Who's Fliegel?" Frank asked.

Stepping forward with a smile, Charlie Brace said, "Don't you know him? Fliegel is the one who followed you from Bayport to Green Sand in his plane."

"The black-eyed character who slithers along like a snake!" Joe exclaimed.

"That's the guy," Charlie continued. "He was in with Flint and Willie long before any of us local chaps got mixed up in the affair. Flint told me the whole story."

"How'd he get started after the oil?" Frank wanted to know.

"Flint used to travel around the country a lot," Charlie explained, "ridin' the rails and scratchin' out a living where he could. He was doin' pretty well in a small town somewhere in the West when he ran into a sick, old wildcatter."

Turk glared at the man who was turning state's evidence, but Charlie continued:

"This old fellow claimed his memory had just returned after a long siege of illness. He was broke, but he said that if Flint would stake him until he could get a job he would tell Flint a tale that might make him rich."

"And Flint believed him?" Joe asked.

"He figured it was worth a gamble," Charlie said. "Anyway, the old man told Flint that fifty years before he had been one of a group of wild-catters who had found a rich deposit of oil. But they had had bad luck. A cave-in buried twenty of 'em. Only the old man escaped."

"So that's what the sign meant," Frank said.

"Yes. The poor wildcatter nailed the sign over his friends' grave. The shock was too much for him, though, and he lost his memory."

All the listeners crowded close around Charlie to hear the fantastic story.

"After Flint had staked him to a place to live and had stocked it with food, the old man led him to the spot—the place you've been callin' Wildcat Swamp. Shortly after that, the poor chap died.

"Before he could do anythin' about the oil, Flint was caught in a train robbery and was sent to prison. That's where he met Willie."

"I wonder why he decided to share the loot with that creep," Joe remarked.

"Well," Charlie said, "I guess he figured Willie would be able to forge the documents to get the land away from Mrs. Sanderson. Then they added Turk because he knew something about engineering."

"How did Snide fit in?" Joe asked with a glance at the glowering captive.

"He was an old friend of Willie and an experienced oil man. They contacted him and he brought Snake Fliegel with him. They gave Snake the job of trying to stop you and Cap Bailey from finding the swamp. He was the one who tampered with your plane so it would crack up before you got off the ground."

"Jack outfoxed them on that one." Joe grinned and saluted Wayne.

"Yes," Charlie said, smiling. "When he flew off and left you at Green Sand Lake, Flint and Turk didn't know what to make of it. They followed you in Fliegel's plane, and Snake was on hand to help them break out of the jail there. Then he piloted them to a field outside Red Butte."

"That's where we came in," one of the rangers spoke up. "We saw his plane land and noticed it had no license number. We investigated and found these cowboy friends of Snide meeting the plane. Our interest must have scared them."

"Right," said another ranger. "They held us at gunpoint, stole our uniforms, and shut us up in that old tower."

"Don't blame it all on us," Turk snapped. "The cowpokes had plenty to do with this deal. They toppled that big boulder over, and sent the fake message to the sheriff's office. Then they called on his wife and fouled up his radiotelephone, returning later to steal it."

Frank and Joe listened intently to this recital, which pieced together various parts of the mystery. A few more questions cleared up the rest of the nefarious plot.

They learned that it was Willie and Snide who had read the story about Bailey's fossil hunt and had held up Cap in his car; it was Snide who had shot down the antenna balloon. The skeleton, Charlie said, had been planted in the cave to scare off intruders.

After congratulating his sons on solving the mystery, Mr. Hardy said, "We ought to go to the fossil pit now and find out how Cap and Chet are."

Several members of the posse were commissioned to take Turk, Snide, and his henchmen off to join Flint and Fliegel in jail.

Then the rest of the group started for the swamp. They had gone about halfway when they met Mrs. Sanderson and Mrs. Paul riding toward them.

"We have good news for you," said Mrs. Sanderson. "Your friends Cap and Chet captured Willie the Penman just as he was trying to force me to sign away my property."

When they heard this news Frank and Joe let out a whoop.

"You have nothing more to fear now," Mr. Hardy told Mrs. Sanderson. "I'll be glad to get a reputable oil company to check on the old wildcatters' theory of a large oil deposit here."

Soon the party reached the foot of the sandy slope in which the camel fossil was buried. There was the sound of pick and shovel from the pit, and in answer to Frank's "Halloo" two heads popped up over the rim.

"I certainly am glad to see you all with a whole skin!" Cap declared as he shook hands with the Hardys.

Frank and Joe grinned. They had indeed

pulled themselves out of a tight fix. Not many weeks were to elapse before they again found their lives in danger while trying to solve the mystery of *The Crisscross Shadow*.

"Wait till we tell you what's happened here," Chet said with pride.

"Now what?" Joe inquired.

"Remember when that first explosion went off? Well, we could feel the earth shaking and heaving way over here. We happened to look down into the old cave, and you should see it now."

"It was like a little earthquake," Cap added. "The explosion opened a subterranean cavern as beautiful as any. It's full of gorgeous stalactites and stalagmites. Mrs. Sanderson, you own a very valuable piece of property even if it turns out that there isn't a drop of oil on it."

"Sure," Chet said, "and we were the first sightseers. Now I qualify for a job as guide."

"A guide!" Joe needled. "You have a job back home—how about that swimming pool?"

"You fellows ran out on me," Chet said reproachfully. "After all the help I've been to you, I should think you'd want to dig it for me."

"I'll help you," offered Cap, "as soon as we dig up my camel fossil."

Chet's eyes shone.

"Frank, Joe, you heard the man!" he exclaimed. "Let's go!"

ORDER FORM

HARDY BOYS MYSTERY SERIES

Now that you've seen Frank and Joe Hardy in action, we're sure you'll want to read more thrilling Hardy Boys adventures. To make it easy for you to purchase other books in this exciting series, we've enclosed this handy order form.

56 TITLES AT YOUR BOOKSELLER
OR COMPLETE AND MAIL THIS
HANDY COUPON TO:

GROSSET & DUNLAP, INC.
P.O. Box 941, Madison Square Post Office, New York, N.Y. 10010

Please send me the Hardy Boys Mystery and Adventure Book(s) checked below @ $2.50 each, plus 25¢ per book postage and handling. My check or money order for $_____ is enclosed.

1.	Tower Treasure	8901-7	28. The Sign of the Crooked Arrow	8928-9
2.	House on the Cliff	8902-5	29. The Secret of the Lost Tunnel	8929-7
3.	Secret of the Old Mill	8903-3	30. Wailing Siren Mystery	8930-0
4.	Missing Chums	8904-1	31. Secret of Wildcat Swamp	8931-9
5.	Hunting for Hidden Gold	8905-X	32. Crisscross Shadow	8932-7
6.	Shore Road Mystery	8906-8	33. The Yellow Feather Mystery	8933-5
7.	Secret of the Caves	8907-8	34. The Hooded Hawk Mystery	8934-3
8.	Mystery of Cabin Island	8908-4	35. The Clue in the Embers	8935-1
9.	Great Airport Mystery	8909-2	36. The Secrets of Pirates Hill	8936-X
10.	What Happened At Midnight	8910-6	37. Ghost at Skeleton Rock	8937-8
11.	While the Clock Ticked	8911-4	38. Mystery at Devil's Paw	8938-6
12.	Footprints Under the Window	8912-2	39. Mystery of the Chinese Junk	8939-4
13.	Mark on the Door	8913-0	40. Mystery of the Desert Giant	8940-8
14.	Hidden Harbor Mystery	8914-9	41. Clue of the Screeching Owl	8941-6
15.	Sinister Sign Post	8915-7	42. Viking Symbol Mystery	8942-4
16.	A Figure in Hiding	8916-5	43. Mystery of the Aztec Warrior	8943-2
17.	Secret Warning	8917-3	44. Haunted Fort	8944-0
18.	Twisted Claw	8918-1	45. Mystery of the Spiral Bridge	8945-9
19.	Disappearing Floor	8919-X	46. Secret Agent on Flight 101	8946-7
20.	Mystery of the Flying Express	8920-3	47. Mystery of the Whale Tattoo	8947-5
21.	The Clue of the Broken Blade	8921-1	48. The Arctic Patrol Mystery	8948-3
22.	The Flickering Torch Mystery	8922-X	49. The Bombay Boomerang	8949-1
23.	Melted Coins	8923-8	50. Danger on Vampire Trail	8950-5
24.	Short-Wave Mystery	8924-6	51. The Masked Monkey	8951-3
25.	Secret Panel	8925-4	52. The Shattered Helmet	8952-3
26.	The Phantom Freighter	8926-2	53. The Clue of the Hissing Serpent	8953-X
27.	Secret of Skull Mountain	8927-0	54. The Mysterious Caravan	8954-8
			55. The Witchmaster's Key	8955-6
			56. The Jungle Pyramid	8956-4

SHIP TO:

NAME _____
(please print)

ADDRESS _____

CITY _____ STATE _____ ZIP _____